COMPLICATIONS

Danielle Steel has been hailed as one of the world's most popular authors, with nearly a billion copies of her novels sold. Her recent international bestsellers include *The Affair*, *Finding Ashley* and *Nine Lives*. She is also the author of *His Bright Light*, the story of her son Nick Traina's life and death; *A Gift of Hope*, a memoir of her work with the homeless; and the children's books *Pretty Minnie in Paris* and *Pretty Minnie in Hollywood*. Danielle divides her time between Paris and her home in northern California.

By Danielle Steel

Complications • Nine Lives • Finding Ashley • The Affair • Neighbours
All That Glitters • Royal • Daddy's Girls • The Wedding Dress
The Numbers Game • Moral Compass • Spy • Child's Play • The Dark Side
Lost And Found • Blessing In Disguise • Silent Night • Turning Point
Beauchamp Hall • In His Father's Footsteps • The Good Fight • The Cast
Accidental Heroes • Fall From Grace • Past Perfect • Fairytale
The Right Time • The Duchess • Against All Odds • Dangerous Games
The Mistress • The Award • Rushing Waters • Magic • The Apartment
Property Of A Noblewoman • Blue • Precious Gifts • Undercover
Country • Prodigal Son • Pegasus • A Perfect Life • Power Play • Winners
First Sight • Until The End Of Time • The Sins Of The Mother
Friends Forever • Betrayal • Hotel Vendôme • Happy Birthday
44 Charles Street • Legacy • Family Ties • Big Girl • Southern Lights
Matters Of The Heart • One Day At A Time • A Good Woman • Rogue
Honor Thyself • Amazing Grace • Bungalow 2 • Sisters • H.R.H.
Coming Out • The House • Toxic Bachelors • Miracle • Impossible • Echoes
Second Chance • Ransom • Safe Harbour • Johnny Angel • Dating Game
Answered Prayers • Sunset In St. Tropez • The Cottage • The Kiss
Leap Of Faith • Lone Eagle • Journey • The House On Hope Street
The Wedding • Irresistible Forces • Granny Dan • Bittersweet
Mirror Image • The Klone And I • The Long Road Home • The Ghost
Special Delivery • The Ranch • Silent Honor • Malice • Five Days In Paris
Lightning • Wings • The Gift • Accident • Vanished • Mixed Blessings
Jewels • No Greater Love • Heartbeat • Message From Nam • Daddy • Star
Zoya • Kaleidoscope • Fine Things • Wanderlust • Secrets • Family Album
Full Circle • Changes • Thurston House • Crossings • Once In A Lifetime
A Perfect Stranger • Remembrance • Palomino • Love: *Poems* • The Ring
Loving • To Love Again • Summer's End • Season Of Passion • The Promise
Now And Forever • Passion's Promise • Going Home

Nonfiction

Expect a Miracle
Pure Joy: *The Dogs We Love*
A Gift Of Hope: *Helping the Homeless*
His Bright Light: *The Story of Nick Traina*

For Children

Pretty Minnie In Hollywood
Pretty Minnie In Paris

Danielle Steel

COMPLICATIONS

MACMILLAN

First published 2021 by Delacorte Press
an imprint of Random House
a division of Penguin Random House LLC, New York

First published in the UK 2021 by Macmillan
an imprint of Pan Macmillan
The Smithson, 6 Briset Street, London EC1M 5NR
EU representative: Macmillan Publishers Ireland Ltd, 1st Floor,
The Liffey Trust Centre, 117–126 Sheriff Street Upper, Dublin 1, D01 YC43
Associated companies throughout the world
www.panmacmillan.com

ISBN 978-1-5290-2164-6

1 3 5 7 9 8 6 4 2

A CIP catalogue record for this book is available from the British Library.

Printed and bound by CPI Group (UK) Ltd, Croydon, CR0 4YY

MIX
Paper from
responsible sources
FSC® C116313

Visit **www.panmacmillan.com** to read more about all our books
and to buy them. You will also find features, author interviews and
news of any author events, and you can sign up for e-newsletters
so that you're always first to hear about our new releases.

To my beloved children,
Beatrix, Trevor, Todd, Nick,
Samantha, Victoria, Vanessa,
Maxx, and Zara,

May every moment of your lives
be precious,
and may your complications
be few, and resolve happily.

I love you so much,
Mom / d.s.

COMPLICATIONS

Chapter 1

T he Louis XVI Hotel on the rue Boissy d'Anglas just off the rue du Faubourg Saint-Honoré in Paris had been closed for renovations for four years. The street it was on was particularly appropriate, open only to foot traffic. It was guarded by a policeman, who would open the barrier for a car to pass carrying an important person, or guests of the exclusive hotel. Smaller than the grand "palaces," the five-star hotels of Paris, it was a favorite among those in the know, the jet set, royalty, and the internationally chic. It had a loyal following of the world's elite, and offered its clients exquisite rooms, enormous suites, all filled with stunning antiques, draperies in the finest silks and satins, beautiful floors reminiscent of Versailles, and a magnificent art collection. Not tiny, and not enormous, it had an intimate feel to it and compared favorably with the many homes of the people who stayed there. It had been flawlessly run with an iron hand by the charming manager Monsieur Louis Lavalle for thirty-eight years. He had been trained at the Ritz, and was famous among hotel guests around the world, and was the envy of his competitors. He was incomparably discreet, and knew all the delicate secrets of the patrons, many movie stars, and people who had much to lose if his mask of secrecy ever slipped. It never had. He didn't allow things to go badly for anyone staying there, no matter how dicey the circumstances. He had been past retirement age, at seventy-four, with no intention of stepping down, when the hotel closed for renovation four years before. A vicious cancer had taken him in its grip halfway through the renovation, and devoured him quickly. Louis Lavalle had succumbed eleven months before the opening. He had run the renovation of the hotel so masterfully that even his death did not delay it. A portrait of him in his formal morning coat had been unveiled the day of the opening, and their old, familiar patrons looked fondly at it as they checked in. There were tears in the eyes of several guests, though not the staff, who respected him, but had often suffered from his rigid diligence. He was every hotel guest's dream, if he deemed them worthy of the Louis XVI. If they didn't live up to the hotel's high standards, they found themselves unable to obtain so much as a lunch reservation there in future, let alone one of the fabulous suites. Indiscretions in the lives of their valued guests were unfailingly overlooked, and M. Lavalle had protected them from the press and paparazzi for years. Bad behavior while at the hotel was not, however, tolerated.

Famous rock stars didn't stand a chance of doing more than passing through the lobby, and even then, they were keenly watched, and met with a chilly greeting. It was not a favorite spot of the famously boorish, and the regulars were forgiven all, which created an unshakable, lasting bond between them and the hotel. The newly rich who didn't know how to behave or respect the premises had never been welcome there. The hotel had been almost fully booked for two years before the reopening. Monsieur Lavalle had noted the first reservations himself. And the fact that he had not lived to see that long-awaited event was a source of grief to all. His standards were almost impossibly high, but he was unfailingly loyal, and he would have given his life to protect the hotel's most faithful guests.

They'd had a few cancellations of the original reservations for the opening, due to death, ill health, or unforeseen circumstances, like divorce or the arrival of a baby right at that time. The last-minute cancellations left room for a few unknowns and new faces among the returning guests. The new manager, Olivier Bateau, would be new to all. The assistant manager had retired after Lavalle's death, unable to conceive of being the adjutant to a less extraordinary general, and had moved to a home in Spain. Louis Lavalle had owned a house in the South of France, and spent his summer vacations there. The perks of the job were numerous and lucrative. He had a son, Albert, whom few people knew about, since he never discussed his personal life. His son was a doctor in Tahiti, married to a local woman there, and had three children. But only the head housekeeper, who had been Louis's discreet companion for twenty years, knew about his son, and it had taken him ten years to tell her. His son never came to Paris, and Lavalle visited him in Tahiti every five or six years. He wasn't close to the boy, who had been brought up by his maternal grandfather in Brittany, after Lavalle and the boy's mother had divorced when his son was barely more than a baby. They were essentially strangers to each other, and Albert was stunned when his father left him his entire estate. He was shocked at the small fortune his father had amassed, and he and his children were set for life, handsomely, from the fruits of his father's labors at the Louis XVI. He meant more to his son in death than he had in life, but Louis would be remembered fondly by him, and with some amazement. He had left his longtime companion, Ghislaine, the head housekeeper, a generous sum too, and she retired to a small, pretty apartment in Cannes shortly after his death. Thanks to Louis, she no longer had to work, and was enjoying her retirement on the Riviera, with fond memories of him.

The third generation of owners of the hotel were consummately discreet and never appeared at the hotel. They remained distant unknown legends and preferred it that way. This latest generation lived in London, and the hotel was a gold mine for them. It had taken Lavalle ten years after they had inherited it to convince them to do the renovation, which was more necessary than the guests realized. Lavalle had convinced the owners at last to add the high-tech features which were essential to their younger clients now. The old guard didn't care about the lack of technology, but Lavalle had recognized that adding it would assure their future. But the new high-tech features still had some bugs in them when the hotel reopened. Technicians were frantically working on it, and it was the last remaining piece of the renovation which was not working smoothly.

They now had a phone system worthy of a space station, and it was well over the head of the new manager, Olivier Bateau, and he was desperately trying to learn how to use it. He went to bed every night with the highly confidential files they kept on all their guests. He knew he had much to learn about many of them. Lavalle had kept many of their profiles safely lodged in his head, and others in the hotel safe.

Bateau's assistant manager, Yvonne Philippe, was new as well. Bateau was forty-one years old, divorced after a brief marriage, like Lavalle himself. He had no children, and had worked at the Hotel du Cap-Eden-Roc for two years at the front desk, and then at the Ritz, where he had done well but had not been considered exceptional. People in hotel circles considered him a dark horse choice, but the owners of the Louis XVI had liked him when they'd met in London. They'd been in a hurry to hire someone after his predecessor's un-timely death a year before the opening. Bateau had never had as much responsibility as he would have now, but they believed that he was capable of handling it, and would be equal to the task in a short time. He was intelligent, eager to please them, and had convinced them that he was the right man for the job.

Bateau had chosen his assistant manager himself. Yvonne Philippe was thirty-two years old, and their paths had crossed at the Ritz, where she had worked for over a year. She was one of the young under-managers at the front desk and seemed like a capable woman. She was a graduate of the École Hôtelière in Lausanne and had worked at the Baur au Lac in Zurich for three years after she gradu-ated. Afterward she had worked at Claridge's in London, and the Four Seasons in Milan. She spoke fluent English, German, Spanish, and Italian, as well as French. Bateau spoke English, German, Rus-sian, and French. Yvonne had a confidence about her, which he liked and reassured him. He suffered from anxiety, and was a worrier by nature, which Yvonne had already figured out about him. He was in a panic over the reopening, and she did everything she could to reassure him. She had an unflappable quality about her. It was valuable in the hotel business, where a crisis could arise at any moment, among highly demanding, spoiled people who wanted their every whim catered to and occasionally got themselves into awkward situations, which they expected the hotel management to solve. Yvonne handled crises of that sort well. Olivier had experienced his share of them at the Ritz, when two major American movie stars had died while staying at the hotel, one of an overdose of heroin, the other of a massive stroke at fifty-seven. There had been several jewel robberies, and serious bomb threats during his tenure there, and various minor diplomatic incidents, all of which had to be handled with the utmost discretion. He had done a good job, but in most cases, had needed the assistance of a senior manager to calm things down. Now he would be that person, and would have to prove himself capable with his assistant manager's backup. She was remarkably resourceful and had dealt with all manner of crises at her previous posts, and already knew some of their regulars from their stays at the hotels where she'd worked in other cities. The regular guests of the Louis XVI were a distinguished crowd, but had many foibles, and were used to having their every whim indulged, which Olivier Bateau was determined to do for them, with Yvonne's help. His secret dream was to become even more of a legend than Louis Lavalle, a very ambitious goal. Unlike Olivier, Lavalle had nerves of steel, and if he was ever frightened or surprised, it never showed.

Still in the first week of the reopening, everything had gone well, with the exception of the Internet, which still had bugs in it, and the phone system, which was continuing to go down in various parts of the hotel with no reasonable explanation. It would come back on a few hours after it went off, as though a ghost were running it and playing tricks on them. Maybe it's Lavalle, Yvonne had suggested. Her superior did not consider it amusing. Why would Lavalle want to torture him, just to remind him that he was still running the show, even from "the other side"? He didn't even like Yvonne saying it in jest, since anything was possible. As Olivier Bateau pointed out to her, hotels had a life and soul of their own, and there were already more than enough superstitions about them. From all he knew of him, he thought Louis Lavalle perfectly capable of haunting the phone system, just to prove a point and make his lingering presence known. Lavalle had acted as though he was the owner of the hotel, and was possessive about it, although people knew he wasn't the owner. But in his discreet way, he had been very grand, and all the new technology had been his idea. Olivier thought it was much more complicated and advanced than necessary for a relatively small hotel.

There were three shops and several vitrines in the lobby. There was the shop of a famous jeweler with a sampling of their very high-end, high-priced wares, a small Loro Piana shop, and a handbag shop carrying various brands, with its own vitrine of vintage Hermès alligator handbags, which sold in the six figures. All of the vitrines were rented by important luxury stores to show a small sample of what was available in their boutiques along the Faubourg. Occasionally they sold a high-priced matching set of jewelry right out of one of the vitrines. People who came to the popular, well-known bar for a drink, or to their famous three-star restaurant, enjoyed looking at the jewelry and other wares in the vitrines. The hotel also had an elaborate alarm system, and a flock of security people to safeguard the merchandise on display.

The prices of the accommodations at the Louis XVI were appropriately high, given the magnificence of the decor and who their guests were, and they had raised their prices again before the reopening. No one of modest means could have afforded to stay there, and people with some of the largest fortunes in Europe, Asia, the Middle East, and a few from America were among their regulars, although the Americans seemed to prefer larger hotels, like the Ritz and the Four Seasons. The more discerning guests had been coming to the Louis XVI for years, and were begging to return now. Sold out by the time they opened, they already had a waiting list for the next four months, and a full house until then. They always kept a small number of rooms and suites in reserve in case someone exceptionally important made a request at the last minute, but even those were in short supply. Halfway through their first week back, Olivier went down the list of people checking in that day, and told Yvonne at an early morning meeting who he wanted her to accompany to their rooms, and who he would be seeing to. All the others could be handled by the junior assistant managers on duty at the front desk.

Yvonne was impressed when Olivier put Gabrielle Gates on her list of people to greet that day. She was on their list of regulars. Yvonne had seen her at Claridge's, but hadn't been allowed to go near her. She was too junior then to greet such an important guest, but as the number two at Louis XVI, despite her age, it was an honor to be allowed to escort such an elite client. Yvonne knew who she was. Gabrielle Gates was American, an important art consultant. Her late father, Theodore Weston, had owned a prominent art gallery in

New York, and she had learned from him. She had been married to Arthur Gates, one of the most successful venture capitalists in the States, who was twenty-five years older than she was. Yvonne vaguely remembered that Gabrielle was around forty-five, had two daughters who were college age or slightly older by then. Gabrielle was a very attractive, very chic woman, with an aura of power around her, her own, and that of her late father and ex-husband. She had been born into a privileged family. Her late mother had been a famously beautiful debutante, and Gabrielle had the self-assurance of a much-loved only child. She was headstrong and had been the apple of her father's eye. Yvonne remembered that there had been a scandal in the last two years when her husband left her for a much younger woman, only three years older than his oldest daughter. There had been a lot of press about it, and talk about how much Arthur Gates was worth, and how young his new bride was. But Gabrielle came from money too, and was a successful art consultant who dealt with extremely high-priced art, and had famous clients. Like all gossip and scandal, the story burned white hot for a while, with photographs of both parties in the press, and after six months the story disappeared.

Gabrielle Gates was famously private and discreet. She had made no comment to the press that hounded her, and eventually they lost interest in her and her story. Arthur had remained visible though, at sixty-eight with his twenty-four-year-old bride, a Russian girl he had met skiing in Saint Moritz.

Yvonne knew her type. The hotels where she worked were full of them, always with much older, very, very rich men. For whatever reason, the men they latched on to were flattered by their attention, and spoiled them beyond belief. Their rejected wives were usually handsomely rewarded with houses and ski chalets, yachts, jewels, planes, and art. The young girls won the big prizes, for however long the relationship lasted, and when it ended, they often found another older man just as wealthy and powerful, or even richer. Yvonne always thought that they certainly knew what they were doing, and she envied them at first, but not for long. She wouldn't have wanted to marry a man like that, or to marry for money. A real Prince Charming would have been welcome, but not a seventy-year-old man and his big bank account. It was all too venal for her. Some of the men with those young girls were pretty awful. She'd never seen Arthur Gates except in photographs, and he was quite a lot older even than his ex-wife. Gabrielle had been his third wife, and he'd been widowed before her. He looked distinguished in photographs, but he was certainly very old, and she didn't think he was a nice man if he had dumped his wife and run off with a gold digger in her early twenties.

She noticed on their reservation lists that Gabrielle had taken their usual suite, and was traveling alone. She had made the reservation fairly recently, and they had done some serious juggling to accommodate her. There were several stars after her name in the old records kept by Louis Lavalle, indicating they should be willing to move heaven and earth to give her the suite she wanted whenever she asked. She came to Paris frequently for business, and to see friends, and the notes said that her husband was always with her. This time obviously, he wasn't. The notes said they had their own plane. It didn't mention who had kept the plane in the divorce. But the car and driver they had hired for her was picking her up at

Charles de Gaulle Airport, not Le Bourget. So, this time she was flying commercial.

When the plane landed at Charles de Gaulle Airport in Roissy, an hour outside Paris, it was the first time Gabrielle had come to Paris in two years. She had stayed at the Ritz and the Four Seasons while the Louis XVI was being renovated, before she and Arthur separated. Neither hotel compared to the smaller, more exclusive hotel she and Arthur loved. She had stayed at the Ritz with her parents as a child when they vacationed in Europe and loved it then, but once she discovered the Louis XVI with Arthur, she had come to prefer the smaller, more personal atmosphere it offered, with its incomparable suites, and their favorite one, and she loved the location so close to the shops on the Faubourg Saint-Honoré.

A year after the hotel had closed, she had discovered Arthur's affair with Sasha. It hadn't remained a secret for long. With the desperation of age, he had become besotted with Sasha, and their affair became a public scandal almost immediately.

There had been no holding their marriage together after the affair hit the media, and he didn't seem to care. Their daughters were furious with him, although now two and a half years later, they hadn't forgiven him, but accepted the situation and saw him anyway. They didn't want to lose their father, even though they thought Sasha was ridiculous and an embarrassment.

For Gabrielle, it had been a crushing blow. She was almost forty-three when she discovered it, and it had hurt immeasurably. They had been married for twenty-two years then. There was no question,

Arthur had a marked preference for young girls, which she no longer was. But this one was a true operator, and he was lavishing a fortune on her, with her expert guidance, haute couture, jewels, a king's ransom in art, which she would sell one day. They had all seen girls like her in operation, but Gabrielle got a view of it this time at close range. She had filed for divorce six months after she discovered the affair. Their divorce had become final a year before her trip to Paris, and had been handled as discreetly as possible. She had dealt with it with dignity, and had refrained from maligning him to their daughters, although she was privately bitter about it. More than bitter, she was crushed. She had thought their love was real and would last forever, and that the twenty-five-year age difference between them would have satisfied his lust for younger women. It hadn't. Sasha had successfully ensnared him. And like many young women of her ilk, she got pregnant as soon as they were married, or possibly just before. The baby boy was three months old now, and Sasha's future was assured. Meanwhile, for the first time in twenty-four years, Gabrielle's future seemed uncertain. Her career was solid and she had continued to work by phone during the whole mess of the divorce, while she attempted to stay out of sight. Her oldest daughter had just moved to L.A. after graduation and her youngest was in college, having fun in Washington at Georgetown University, as a senior. Both girls were upset by Arthur's infant son. Gabrielle hadn't quite recovered from it either, although she wasn't surprised, given who and what Sasha was, a gold digger of the most efficient kind, and damn good at it, a real pro. The whole thing was humiliating in the extreme.

It didn't matter to her that Arthur looked foolish to everyone, but it did matter that there were men among his peers who envied him, men whom she realized now had never really been her friends. She had been disposed of and forgotten, and she was glad that her parents were no longer alive to see it. They had lavished love on her as an only child, born to them as a surprise late in life. She knew that watching her get cast away by Arthur would have broken their hearts, nearly as much as it had hers, and her daughters'. It was small comfort to know that her father would have been livid at Arthur. She felt undesirable, old, and vulnerable now nonetheless. She covered it well, and remained calm, cool, and professional with her clients, but she felt broken inside, and didn't even let her daughters see to what extent. For months, she had cried all the time whenever she was alone. She felt dazed, and hopeless about the future. She saw herself suddenly middle-aged at forty-three when she filed for divorce, and had no desire to start her life again. It had taken her more than two years to get back on her feet. No one had seen her socially since the divorce. She had stopped traveling, except to go to the most important art fairs, and only did that when she had to, to meet a client. She never made any reference whatsoever to Arthur and his new wife and child. And no one would have dared bring the subject up with her.

Therapy with a good psychiatrist, medication for a few months, time, her love for her daughters, and her work ethic had finally pulled her out of it. Gabrielle had inherited her elegance from her mother, and her passion for art from her father. Both traits had helped her survive. The trip to Paris was a somewhat last-minute decision. She opted to come to Paris for the Biennale antique furniture and art show in September, and an important Sotheby's auction, which coincided perfectly with the reopening of what had been her and Arthur's favorite hotel. She was curious to see it, although a little worried about what ghosts would linger there for her. She hadn't been able to resist the urge to ask for their usual suite, and was afraid doing so might have been a mistake. She just prayed that Arthur and Sasha weren't going to the Biennale too, but she didn't think they would. Sasha's tastes were less sophisticated, and Gabrielle knew she preferred contemporary art. Arthur had spent a fortune buying the most expensive, avant-garde artwork for her.

Gabrielle flew commercial for the first time in years, since Arthur had kept the plane. She hadn't wanted it. She was simply dressed when she emerged from the flight, in black jeans and loafers, a plain black sweater and fur jacket, and a large black leather Hermès Birkin bag she used for travel. Her face was beautiful, and she was slim and tall, with creamy white skin, very dark hair pulled tightly back, and big green eyes. But you had to look carefully to spot her. She liked disappearing quietly into a crowd, and not being noticed, despite her striking looks. It was only once you did that you saw her aristocratic bearing, her quiet grace, and all the trappings of natural elegance. She was a woman who didn't like to be in the limelight and even less so now. There had been a time, when she was first married to Arthur, that she let him show her off like a beautiful doll, but she was never comfortable with it, and over the years grew into her own simple chic style. And now he had the dolly he had always wanted, a girl he could dress up and show off, oblivious to her vulgarity and content to highlight her youth, while she bled him for everything she could get out of him. Gabrielle had never done anything like that to him. She loved him, had inherited her own money, and had never been after Arthur's. He was in a very different situation now. Gabrielle had dignity and grace, unlike Sasha, who was common and cunning, and very sexy.

A ground crew agent from Air France met Gabrielle at the plane, helped her at baggage claim, and turned her over to the driver with a discreet black Mercedes the hotel had sent for her. Arthur had bought Sasha a silver Bentley. He drove a Lamborghini himself. Arthur liked the luxuries his success provided, and so did Sasha. Gabrielle didn't care about that, although she had flown first class, with the curtain of her compartment drawn so she could have privacy. It was comfortable that way, and she skipped dinner and slept on the flight. Always fashionably thin, she was too much so now. It had been a hard two and a half years in her life, and she was looking forward to staying at her favorite hotel again, as though everything would be fine when she got there, thinking mistakenly that she could turn back the clock. Gabrielle knew she couldn't, and kept telling herself she was better off, if this was who Arthur really was. More than anything, she was disappointed, but she didn't want anyone's pity, which was why she had stayed away from everyone she knew, and had known during her marriage. She neither wanted to malign the man she had loved, nor lament him, or feel sorry for herself.

She knew she would have a good life without him, and reminded herself of it constantly. Intelligently, and reasonably, she knew she would be okay, but it still hurt at times. This trip was the first evidence of her new life, and of her courage to go back to familiar places without him. She wasn't sure if she had bitten off more than she should have, but if it turned out to be too much for her, she could always leave, and go home, or move to the Ritz.

As they drove toward Paris, she didn't feel shaky, she felt brave, and was glad she had taken the trip. She loved Paris, and didn't want to give it up for him. He didn't own it, nor did Sasha. They had each other now. That was enough.

The Louis XVI had kept most of their employees on partial salary during the renovation. Only the more recent hires had been let go entirely and some of the long-term employees were paid in full and waited to return when the hotel reopened. The doorman recognized Gabrielle immediately, and greeted her warmly, lifting his cap as she smiled. He took charge of her luggage, and she went through the revolving door, and headed to the front desk.

She noticed immediately that at first glance, the hotel had changed very little. The signature pieces of art and furniture were seemingly unchanged and placed in the same locations. A new carpet had been woven with the exact same design as the old one, but here and there she saw shiny new marble, and more modern-looking vitrines for the jewelry.

The red uniforms of the bellboys were the same as they had been for decades but were all new, as were the fresh-faced boys wearing them, many of them too young to shave and barely more than teenagers. And the lineup of faces at the reception desk was all brand new too. She recognized no one, which surprised her a little. She thought she'd see one or two of the old guard, although she knew that M. Lavalle had died, and his assistant and the head housekeeper had retired. What she saw instead was a nervous-looking balding man in his forties who looked flustered. She introduced herself, and he did the same, and said he was Olivier Bateau, the new manager. He welcomed her, but wasn't impressed by how she was dressed. He was used to the outer trappings of more ostentatious, less discreet guests, and pawned her off on his assistant, Yvonne Philippe, immediately, and said Miss Philippe would take her to her room. It was the first major change, since Louis Lavalle had always personally escorted them to their suite. But she wondered if it was because she was no longer married to Arthur, and attributed it to that more than anything else.

Gabrielle was tired after the overnight flight, and Yvonne was quiet and respectful as they walked through the lobby so familiar to Gabrielle. She noticed small changes all along the way, but no major ones. They had done the remodeling well and as much as possible they'd kept things close to the original version that everyone loved. The elevator was all marble and mirror now, and looked less Old World but reassuringly modern and efficient, although they still had a liveried man to run it, which wasn't needed. Yvonne explained the new high-tech features available in every room now, and admitted quietly that they were still "working out a few details" with the Internet and phones, but expected everything to be working smoothly within a day or two. Gabrielle was planning to stay for a week.

Gabrielle held her breath as Yvonne unlocked the room with a new electronic key system, and when the door to the suite opened as though by magic. At first glance, everything looked the same. She could see that all the fabrics were new, but the furniture and the color scheme remained unchanged in a soft pale sky blue. There were satins and brocades everywhere, and the new curtains were magnificent, better than the old ones. They had replaced the Aubusson carpet with another one, but the effect was as handsome as it had been before. On closer inspection, there were some new pieces

19

of furniture in the room, all antiques, and a new mirrored mini bar. The carved white marble mantelpiece that she and Arthur had loved was still there. The bathrooms in the suite, two full ones and a powder room, were stunningly modern now and very grand, but with an antique feel to them. Yvonne explained all the technology in the room then, and showed her how to work everything on an iPad, including the curtains.

It was the best remodel Gabrielle had ever seen, rather like her own. She had considered a facelift when Arthur left her, and fortunately the plastic surgeon she consulted talked her out of it and said she didn't need it. Instead he suggested some injections, filler, some subtle changes, and an electrical treatment to "surprise" her face back to youth. The results had been very successful. She didn't look different or as though she had had work done. The changes were very subtle and made her look rested and healthy and highlighted her features. It made her look more beautiful, and took a full decade off her age in her appearance. She smiled, thinking that she and the hotel had been subtly rejuvenated, without doing anything too invasive or destructive. Her daughters hadn't even noticed the changes to her face until months after she'd had them. But with Arthur's new wife being nineteen years younger than she was, she felt so old that she wanted to do something, and was glad she had. It had been the beginning of her starting to lead a new life on her own. And this was the second big step, coming to Paris by herself.

She gave Yvonne a handsome tip, and her bags arrived in the suite before the assistant manager left. Yvonne had noticed how surprised Gabrielle looked when Olivier didn't take her to her room, which Yvonne thought was a mistake, but Gabrielle had been very pleasant to her, and was too polite to object to what was actually a step down in how she was treated at the hotel. The new manager didn't know any better, which Yvonne thought was a concern, but Gabrielle didn't make an issue of it.

A few minutes later Gabrielle was alone in the suite with a pyramid of macarons prepared by the chef, a plate of strawberries, a bowl of fruit, a massive box of the best chocolates, a huge bouquet of pink roses, and a bottle of their favorite champagne chilling, Dom Pérignon, which they preferred to Cristal, their standard offering to important Americans.

Gabrielle sat down in a chair and looked around the suite. It hadn't changed significantly, but everything else in her life had, and she had. Arthur was gone now, in the arms of his new wife. Gabrielle had lived the life of a recluse for the past few years, although she had promised her therapist that she would try to get out more, and this trip was a major step. It was amazing to think how her life had changed in four years, during the hotel renovation. Her daughters had grown up, one had left home and the other was in college. They had started their own lives, so she was truly alone now, as never before. And being in Paris, in the room where she and Arthur had been so happy so many times over the years, seemed to underline it as nothing else could have. It brought tears to her eyes as she stood up and looked out the window at the rooftops of the Faubourg Saint-Honoré. Well-constructed double windows kept the noise out and a new air-conditioning system, also operated from the iPad, had been added. She knew that she just had to go forward now. She was sad for a minute, but was well aware that that wouldn't change anything, and she didn't want to give depression a chance to take hold.

She glanced at her watch, and decided to walk through the Biennale, see which galleries were represented, and to check out their booths anonymously, strolling through the elaborate exhibition at the Grand Palais. Some vendors spent as much as a million dollars on their booths, and she wanted to see them. She opened the champagne and poured herself a glass, helped herself to a macaron from the pyramid of them on the silver tray, and tried not to think about Arthur. He was no longer part of her life, and didn't deserve to be. She was in Paris, at her favorite hotel, and both she and the hotel had changed for the better. It was all she allowed herself to think about, as she washed her face and brushed her long dark hair. She had her life ahead of her, and she was going to make it a good life, whatever it took. She headed toward the lobby ten minutes later, on the way to the Biennale, and she was smiling. She was happy to be there.

Chapter 2

As Gabrielle Gates slid into the Mercedes with the driver the hotel had hired for her for the duration of her stay, she saw a tall, gray-haired man arrive in a dark suit with a stern face. He got out of a taxi, carrying a briefcase and a small rolling bag, which he carried himself, and she noticed that the doorman made a fuss about him. He never smiled, but everything about him suggested that he was important. He looked very severe, preoccupied, and unhappy. He never smiled at the doorman, and walked hurriedly into the hotel. Her driver noticed him too.

"Who was that?" she asked, curious about him. She had requested an English-speaking driver, since she didn't speak French, but understood bits and snatches of it after years of doing business with the art world in France. Arthur hadn't spoken it either. "Is he someone important? The doorman looked impressed."

"He is important," the driver confirmed, as he glanced at her in the rearview mirror. The driver was about her age, and was well dressed in a black suit, white shirt, and black tie, and spoke good English. "He's Patrick Martin, our minister of the interior. He's going to run for president in the elections next spring." He looked to be somewhere in his fifties, and now that the driver mentioned it, there was something presidential about him. It was easy to believe.

"Do you think he'll win?" She was intrigued by him. He didn't look like much fun, but he looked serious and respectable.

"Maybe so. Maybe not on the first round, but on the second one. Our presidential election is in two parts. He's very well respected, although not very warm. But maybe we would be better off with a not warm president, who is a serious person. Some of the amusing ones have been bad presidents. And power goes to their heads, for all of them. Then they bring their girlfriends and mistresses and scandals to the Élysée. Patrick Martin has no scandals. He's very . . . rigid, do you say? And very pure."

"He looks it," Gabrielle said, amused by the driver's description of him.

"We have many parties in France. He will run against two women. One is a Communist, and the other one very right wing and extreme. He would be better. But there are some others too."

"Politics are confusing everywhere these days," she said, looked at the pamphlet she had of the galleries showing at the Biennale and forgot about the minister of the interior. She wondered why he was staying at the hotel. Maybe he was meeting a woman. He had entered the hotel at full speed.

* * *

When Patrick Martin got to the front desk at the Louis XVI, he asked for Olivier Bateau by name. He had made the reservation himself, and Olivier saw him arrive and approached immediately.

"It's a great honor to meet you, Minister," Olivier said a little grandly, and Patrick looked uncomfortable. He had already told him on the phone that he wished to be discreet. Hotel managers were used to those requests and guessed immediately the reason for them.

"Is my room ready?" Patrick responded. He had asked for a simple room, with no fanfare. He had said he would be using it for a meeting, which Olivier didn't believe. An assignation with a woman was more likely. Martin was a handsome man.

"Of course. I'll take you up myself." Bateau came around the front reception desk rapidly, with electronic key in hand. He had spent more time at the front desk than in his office for the past week. He wanted to be there to greet their more important guests when they arrived. He had missed the boat with Gabrielle Gates and still didn't realize it. Yvonne did, since she had seen the VIP reception Gabrielle had gotten both at Claridge's and the Four Seasons in Milan, when she worked there. She knew they had fallen short at the Louis XVI, but Gabrielle had been extremely polite about it and hadn't complained.

Patrick Martin and the manager got into the elevator together, Olivier had requested the third floor, one of their VIP floors, with the grander suites. He stepped out ahead of Patrick and led the way. He opened the door and waved Patrick into the room. The minister looked shocked the moment he walked in, and turned to Olivier with a look of displeasure.

"I asked for a simple room. This is an enormous, luxurious suite." He looked anything but happy about it.

"Indeed, sir. We upgraded you, at no extra charge. It is our pleasure to give you one of our finest suites." Olivier looked delighted with himself. The minister of the interior didn't.

"Can you switch me back to a plain room, not a suite?"

Olivier was shocked and disappointed. "I'm afraid not, sir. We're completely full for the next several weeks. And many people have specifically requested their old rooms. I hope you'll be happy here, sir." He had expected Patrick to be over the moon. Instead he seemed agitated, and his already thin lips were set in a straight line.

"Fine. It's only for one night. It doesn't sit well for a minister to indulge himself with such luxury, even though I'm paying for it myself." He had used a personal credit card when he checked in at the desk, not his government one. "I'm expecting you to be discreet," he reiterated to Olivier.

"Of course, sir. That's understood." Normally, they would expect to know if the room would be occupied by more than one person, but under no circumstance did he intend to ask the minister of the interior that question. The minister of the interior was responsible for secret government agencies, like the FBI and CIA in the States. He was a powerful man. He stood uncomfortably, looking around the suite, obviously eager for the manager to leave, which he did hastily. Patrick sat down heavily in an antique Louis XVI armchair and sighed. He felt anxious just being there. He opened his briefcase and glanced into it, and then checked the rolling bag. He had everything he needed. He felt tense and unable to relax while he waited, and then finally stood up, walked over to the mini bar, and poured himself a stiff drink of straight scotch, neat. He drank it down, poured himself a second one, and took it with him to sit and wait for the knock on the door.

When Olivier Bateau got back to the front desk after seeing Patrick Martin to his room, a tall, distinguished, burly man was checking in. He looked serious, but he had warm, friendly eyes. He was somewhere in his late forties, spoke French fluently with a British accent, and said his name was Alaistair Whyte-Jones. He said he had reserved a junior suite, which was a bedroom with a sitting area, no separate living room. It was a new configuration since the remodel, and they had several of them. He said he had never stayed there before, which they had already noted about him in the computer.

He didn't explain why to them, but he had a meeting in Paris, and had decided to treat himself to a few days' holiday, which he hadn't had in a long time. Paris was his favorite city, and he was happy to be there. He looked around the hotel and was led to his room by one of the young junior managers at the front desk.

There was nothing in Mr. Whyte-Jones's file to indicate that he was a VIP, and he didn't act like one. He behaved like an ordinary person, intelligent, businesslike, with good manners, to whom a few days at the Louis XVI was a special event, not a regular occurrence, and he probably wouldn't be back soon. He was checking in alone, and he looked strikingly British, a tweed jacket that looked like it had been made by a reasonably good tailor, gray slacks, dark brown suede shoes. He looked like an English country gentleman, but he wasn't a lord, or anyone out of the ordinary, so he warranted no special treatment from the manager, nor his assistant. He seemed perfectly content to go to his room with the young woman walking beside him with the key. For him, it was exciting enough just being here. He never stayed at hotels like this, but had decided to treat himself to a brief stay in a fancy hotel. He had read about the Louis XVI and wanted to see it for himself, firsthand. He was only sorry he didn't have anyone to share the experience with. But he was grateful to be there, and was savoring it.

A young American couple checked in shortly after Alaistair Whyte-Jones. They had a jubilant, almost euphoric look about them, and Yvonne wondered if they were on their honeymoon, but didn't ask. The last names on their passports were different, which didn't mean anything, since if this was their honeymoon, they wouldn't have had time to change the name on her passport yet. And these days so many women didn't change their names when they married, particularly Americans. They looked as though they were celebrating something, when a bellboy in his new uniform with the traditional red cap and red jacket took them to their room. They looked conspiratorial, but not guilty, and above all they looked happy. It made Yvonne smile to watch them, as they disappeared into the elevator with the bellboy and she saw them kiss. They weren't in the first blush of youth either. She had seen on their passports that he was thirty-eight years old, and she was thirty-nine, so they knew what they were doing, whatever it was. She had no way of knowing that their story was worthy of a novel or a TV show.

Richard Sheffield had met Judythe at her wedding two years before. He was a college friend of the groom's, no longer particularly close to the groom, but for old time's sake the groom had invited him to the wedding. They had been roommates in a big house during their last year at the University of New Hampshire. Judythe worked in the advertising department of a magazine in New York, and had waited until thirty-seven to marry. The right guy just hadn't come along, and she finally convinced herself that she didn't need the perfect match to get married. The groom was a stock analyst on Wall Street. He had a good job. They seemed compatible, had a good time together, and liked the same sports. She decided that was good enough before she missed her chance completely. They had broken up a couple of times, when she wanted to meet someone more exciting. The man she was marrying wasn't exciting, but he was solid and a decent guy. Richard had been married to a nurse for three years, and they didn't have children yet. He was an editor and writer at a travel magazine.

Lightning struck at the wedding. Richard and Judythe talked and bells went off, for both of them. They didn't dare say anything to each other, and Judythe told herself it was because they'd all been drinking. He danced with her then, and it was like an electrical current between them. She had never been as attracted to anyone in her life, and certainly not the man she had just married. They both did their best to ignore it. Her honeymoon in Wyoming was fun, but as soon as she got back, all she could think about was Richard. He called her for lunch, and it was like fireworks between them all over again, cold sober this time, and with no dancing.

Three lunches and two months after she'd gotten married, she wound up in a hotel room with Richard. They both felt guilty about it, but couldn't stop. She knew she'd made a terrible mistake getting married, and Richard had come to the same conclusion about his own marriage, months after his wedding. The woman he had married complained constantly, didn't think his job was good enough, had no imagination, hated to travel, and spent all her spare time in New Jersey with her sisters. It took him less than six months to realize he didn't love her. It crystallized for both of them when Richard and Judythe met at her wedding, and Judythe felt like a liar and a cheat with her husband.

They'd been married for five months when she told him she had made a terrible mistake and he deserved better. She tried not to tell him about Richard, but it came out eventually. And Steve Oakes, her husband, was a gentleman about it. He was devastated, but they both agreed that it was better to face it sooner than later. She filed the divorce a few weeks later, and was divorced in a year.

Richard's took longer. His wife went after him like a cat when he told her he wanted out. He couldn't see himself having children with her. They had both made a terrible mistake. She wanted to turn the mistake into an income, and went after him financially. He finally paid her a settlement for her "pain and suffering," and his divorce had just become final a month earlier.

He'd been reading about the Louis XVI reopening in Paris, and he pulled every string he could to get a discount as a travel writer, and book the least expensive room possible at the Louis XVI. It was still way out of their budget, but they had something to celebrate after everything they'd been through. They were planning to get married eventually, but didn't have plans yet. They'd been living together since they had both separated. But both divorces had taken all their energy and his money. Coming to Paris to celebrate their divorces was a big deal. They were planning to spend four days at the Louis

XVI, and then spend a weekend in Rome at a hotel that had comped them. Judythe had never been so happy in her life, nor had Richard. It had been a hell of a fight, but they had been brave and honest, and their dreams had finally come true. And what better place to celebrate it than Paris? Judythe had never stayed at a hotel like it in her entire life. And whatever came after this would be icing on the cake. To top it off, right before the trip, Richard had been given a big promotion at the magazine, and a raise. They wanted to do some traveling, and they couldn't wait to have kids.

Gabrielle Gates checked out the Biennale that afternoon, and made due note of where the various galleries were that she was interested in at the exhibition in the Grand Palais. She ordered tea from room service when she returned, and sat back to relax in the living room of the beautiful suite. After the initial pang of nostalgia when she walked in, the room was beginning to seem more like her own now than a sacred place she and Arthur had shared. Arthur had violated all those memories without sentiment, so why should she consider the hotel sacred to them now? Why should she be sad about it? She had come here to kick-start her new life. She was here now and wanted to make it good and not waste a minute of it. This was her time now. She felt she had earned it after her husband broke her heart.

Alaistair Whyte-Jones opened a window, lit a cigar, and poured himself a brandy. He'd decided to relax at the hotel and enjoy his room for a while before he went out. The junior suite was more elegant than he had expected, and he was only sorry he didn't know anyone in Paris to invite over to see it. He made a call to a number on a business card he took out of his wallet and confirmed an appointment for the next day. He didn't know the man he was meeting, but a mutual friend had gotten Alaistair the appointment.

Richard and Judythe had planned to go out and walk around Paris, but got waylaid by their bed and a bottle of champagne that had been left for them in their room. They wound up making love for several hours, before going for a long walk, arm in arm, down the Faubourg Saint-Honoré, and eventually ended up in the Tuileries Gardens, and sat on a bench kissing. Neither of them could believe that they had a whole life together now, and nothing could stop them. All the bad stuff and the legal issues were behind them. They had corrected their mistakes, paid their dues, and now it was smooth sailing ahead.

They ate dinner at a little bistro before they went back to the hotel and made love again. Life had never seemed more perfect. And what better place to celebrate it than Paris? They had dealt with all the complications in their lives, and the trip was their reward for it. They knew that this time, when they married, it wouldn't be a mistake, for either of them.

Olivier Bateau had begun to relax, sitting in his office behind the front desk. He could breathe again when Yvonne walked in and reported that all was well in their world, except that the phone system still appeared to be failing at times, but a team was working on it, and promising it would be fixed shortly.

"Except for the phones, all is peaceful," she said, smiling at him, as he shook his head.

"For the moment," he added. "That could change in an instant. Hotels are complicated. They're like living, breathing beings, with a mind and life of their own." She had already learned that he was a pessimist, wracked by anxiety, and he always saw doom lurking around the corner.

"I think for a first week, things have gone pretty damn well," she said. He hesitated and then nodded. It made him think of the minister of the interior in the glorious suite they had upgraded him to. Olivier couldn't help wondering who Patrick Martin was meeting there that night, and there was no doubt in his mind whatsoever that he was cheating on his wife. And whoever it was, Olivier was glad they had given him the big suite. He was sure that when Patrick became president, he would remember it.

Chapter 3

P atrick Martin paced the room periodically, while he waited for the person he was meeting to arrive. He stood at the window several times, but remained concealed by the filmy curtains, so he wasn't in plain sight. He had finished two scotches by the time he heard a knock on the door. He had texted the room number, and told his guest to walk straight to the elevator, and not make inquiries at the front desk. Patrick had received a brief "Okay" in response. He felt certain that everyone at the desk would be too busy to notice a self-assured stranger arrive, and wouldn't stop him.

When the knock finally came, Patrick opened the door quickly, and a breathtakingly handsome, truly beautiful, graceful young man entered. He was in his early twenties. He was Russian, and had trained as a dancer in Moscow at the state school. Since arriving in Paris three years before, he had been modeling, not dancing. He was strikingly good-looking with straight blond hair to his shoulders, and an exquisite body with every muscle rippling. When Patrick looked at him, he felt the same things he always did, fierce, overwhelming attraction, anger, and revulsion all at once. His attraction to Sergei Karpov made him feel like a prisoner. As Patrick watched him move with the stealth of a cat, or a long, lean leopard, Sergei smiled at him, reached for the bottle of champagne in the ice bucket, opened it, poured two glasses and handed one to Patrick.

"I like the room," he said with a wicked smile, as Patrick refused the champagne.

"I'll stick with scotch." Sergei shrugged, to indicate he didn't care. "They upgraded me," Patrick said.

"You're an important man," Sergei confirmed, as he continued to prowl and investigate the room, opening things and closing them, while Patrick sat looking uncomfortable and watched him. You never knew what Sergei would do next. "You're especially important now that you've decided to run for president next year."

"That's not entirely sure yet. It was foolish to come here. It's too showy, and too public. We should have met somewhere else. I thought they'd be too busy with the opening to notice us." But the upgrade proved otherwise.

"Bad hotels depress me. I deserve this. So do you." Patrick didn't comment. Sergei seemed totally at home as he settled in a Louis XVI chair, his long, graceful legs stretched out in front of him. He reached for the phone then, and before Patrick could stop him, he called room service and ordered foie gras, caviar, and vodka, and smiled at Patrick when he hung up. "I'm starving." As he said it, he reached over and grabbed Patrick roughly and kissed him. He taunted and tantalized him, which was his stock in trade, as he pulled off Patrick's clothes and his own. Sergei was an expert at sexual delights, which Patrick knew only too well.

He could never resist him, and a minute later, they were naked on the bed, which Sergei had pulled open, and engaged in brutal, raw, animal sex, as both men made guttural sounds, and Sergei finally roared like a lion. It had been quick and violent, as always. They had barely finished when the room service waiter rang the doorbell, and Patrick shoved Sergei roughly toward the bathroom, dumped their clothes on the floor, and grabbed a terry-cloth hotel robe. He looked disheveled and severe when he opened the door and let the waiter in, told him to leave everything on the rolling table, signed for it hastily, and prayed that Sergei wouldn't come out before the waiter had left. Sergei was unpredictable, wild and unmanageable, which made him even more irresistible. He knew better than to come out, and waited until he heard the door close behind the waiter. He strolled out naked, with his spectacular body in full view, and helped himself to the caviar and foie gras, and then poured himself a glass of the chilled vodka. He offered some to Patrick, who shook his head. He wasn't enjoying the performance, but Sergei clearly was. Every minute of it. He knew he was in full control of Patrick, and had been for two years. It was an agonizing relationship of sex, hatred, and lust.

He glanced at Patrick then and asked him, "Did you bring it?" Patrick nodded, sitting in the robe, looking miserable. "Where is it?" He pointed to his briefcase. "Bring it to me," Sergei commanded in a silky voice. Patrick hesitated, with a defeated expression, got up, brought the briefcase to Sergei, and handed it to him. Sergei smiled broadly, both at the subservience, and at the prospect of what Patrick had brought. He opened the briefcase, and took out neat stacks of euros, set them on the table, and counted them, still naked and unbearably beautiful. He made every gesture a sexual act that was excruciating to watch and aroused Patrick immediately, just as it had since they met.

"It's all there," Patrick said in a low growl.

"It is and it isn't. I've been thinking," Sergei said. "We agreed on that amount before you decided to run for president. You're worth a great deal more now. You're a very, very important man. I want more." Patrick looked ill as Sergei smiled evilly at him.

"I can't get more. I had to tell a million lies and call in favors to get that much cash. Between the bank and my wife, I have nowhere else to pull it from. This is all I can do." There was desperation in Patrick's face and voice. His relationship with the young Russian came at a high price.

"And just think of what you'll be worth to me once you're the president," Sergei said and laughed.

"For God's sake," Patrick said, exploding at him, "how long do you expect this to go on?"

"As long as it has to. Besides, we haven't stopped. Every time you see me, you want me, and we do it again." There were tears in Patrick's eyes as he listened. He was trapped by this vicious young blackmailer with no morals whatsoever and his desire for him. "And if you don't want to pay me more, I think your wife, and the media, would be very interested in this story, don't you?"

Patrick lunged at him in fury and Sergei leapt lightly away, laughing at him. He wasn't afraid of Patrick's rage. Sergei was faster, younger, and more cunning. He was half Patrick's age. Patrick suddenly couldn't take it anymore, the constant pressure, the threats, the demands for ever more money that Patrick could no longer meet. He had squeezed money from every possible source to pay Sergei. If he did it anymore, he would be exposed, and could lose everything. He had put everything he cared about at risk. He was married, had children, planned to run for high office, and if his secret homosexual escapades were exposed, it would ruin him, end his marriage and destroy his career. Sergei knew it. He was taking full advantage of Patrick's vulnerability and had since the first time they'd had sex two years before, in the dark bathroom of a gay bar in a dangerous neighborhood.

Sergei taunted Patrick, dancing away from him, getting away from him with ease, as he moved backward as though on air. Patrick became more and more enraged, and lunged at him again. There was no plan to his actions. He was maybe going to push him, hoping to intimidate him, not hurt him. Patrick wasn't a violent man, but he was trembling with frustration. Sergei had pressed him to his limits. Sergei suddenly looked startled. He had tripped over a little stool that had been shoved out of place when Patrick chased him. Sergei flew backward gracefully, as Patrick watched him. Sergei almost floated, his body arched as he crashed to the floor and landed flat on his back with his arms outstretched.

There was silence in the room, after Patrick's agonized shouts of anger a few minutes earlier. He stood staring at Sergei, as blood ran from his nostrils and mouth, his eyes filled with blood, and in a moment there was a pool of blood around his head. Patrick stared at him in terror and revulsion. It was obvious that Sergei was dead. His blood-filled eyes were open and stared straight ahead. The part of the floor he was lying on was marble, which was unforgiving. The little stool he fell over lay on its side, overturned. And even as he lay there dead, he looked graceful.

Leaving Sergei lying in his own blood, spreading around him, Patrick reached for the bundles of euros on the table and shoved them back in his briefcase. He didn't touch Sergei or try to cover him or move him. He had no idea what to do now. He had never intended to kill him, or even hurt him. All he wanted to do now was run, but he had to think first. He flipped the switch at the door of the room to signal "do not disturb" with a red light in the hall. Patrick was panicked. This would ruin him. He had accidentally killed the man he'd had sex with and who was blackmailing him. Patrick dressed hurriedly, and approached to stare at Sergei again. Patrick was crying out of sheer terror, as the pool of blood around Sergei continued to spread.

In her suite, Gabrielle was studying the room service menu, trying to decide what to eat. She tried to call room service, but the phone in her room was dead, which was annoying. She wasn't really hungry, and ate a piece of fruit from the bowl on the table instead, wondering when the phone would be fixed.

In his room, Alaistair was enjoying his brandy and cigar, savoring the peaceful moment.

Complications

* * *

Richard and Judythe were in the bathtub, surrounded by candle-light, talking about their plans for the future, and what they were going to do in Rome that weekend. This was pure heaven. When they got out of the bath, they made love again, and afterward, as Judythe said something to Richard, he suddenly clutched his chest, made a strange noise, and his eyes rolled back in his head. Judythe looked at him in panic.

"Richard! Talk to me! What's happening?" He slipped deep into unconsciousness. Judythe tried to shake him, and reached for the phone to call for help. The phone was dead. She then grabbed one of the hotel robes, put it on, and pulled Richard as gently as she could off the bed, got him on the floor, dragged him close to the door where she could call for help and someone might hear her. She remembered that from a first-aid class she'd taken. She pulled the door open, and checked him again. He wasn't breathing, and had no pulse. With the door open, she shouted for help. There was no one in the hallway to hear her. She screamed as loudly as she could, feeling desperate, and started chest compressions, while begging him not to leave her. She was keeping him alive with the chest compressions. There was no sign of anyone to help them, and she continued to scream and shout, praying someone would hear. She was crying but never lost the rhythm of the compressions.

In his room across the hall, Alaistair thought he heard a woman screaming, but it couldn't be. Not here at this hotel. He thought it must be the TV. But he heard it again, desperate cries for help, in English, the sound of a woman's voice. He opened the door of his suite, directly across from Richard and Judythe's room, saw her giving him chest compressions, and instantly picked up the phone in his room to call the front desk for help. The phone in his room was dead too, and he rushed into the hall, grabbed a defibrillator from the wall, and went to Richard and Judythe immediately.

"I'm a doctor," he told her, as he opened the kit and handed her his cellphone, and told her how to call the SAMU, the French emergency medical services, and what to say. Someone at the other end knew enough English to understand her, and Richard's heart started from the defibrillator, and then stopped again. Alaistair started chest compressions again. Judythe watched in desperation. Gabrielle heard something in the hallway, as Judythe screamed for help again. Gabrielle came out of her room to see what it was. She heard voices raised, as Judythe frantically talked to Richard, and Alaistair continued trying to revive him, or at least keep him alive until the SAMU could show up.

When Gabrielle realized what was happening, she hurried to them and said to Alaistair, "What can I do?" He remained calm, and looked straight at Gabrielle. The seriousness of the situation was obvious.

"Go down to the front desk and tell them what's happening, and get the SAMU up here as soon as they arrive." Gabrielle headed for the stairs as fast as she could, and arrived at the front desk as Olivier was desperately trying to calm guests complaining loudly that their phones weren't working. They had come downstairs to complain. Several sections of phones were dead. He assured them that the problem would be fixed shortly, as Gabrielle interrupted them all.

"There's a man who has had a heart attack on the third floor. The SAMU is coming. We need help."

"There's a defibrillator on the wall in the hallway," Olivier said as he came out from behind the front desk, and left the irate guests to Yvonne, who had been about to leave for the day. Now she would have to stay, with the phone system down, and a heart attack on the third floor. She would escort the SAMU upstairs when they came.

"There's a doctor with him," Gabrielle explained, as they ran to the elevator and got out on the third floor. "The defibrillator didn't work."

"Then he's dead," Olivier said bluntly.

"No, he's not. The doctor is doing CPR on him, and keeping his heart pumping." They saw the same scene continuing as they reached the doorway of Richard and Judythe's room. Alaistair was doing chest compressions, and Judythe was giving him all the information she could, that Richard was thirty-eight years old, and had no history of heart trouble.

"Could it be something else?" she asked Alaistair, and he shook his head.

"Unlikely. No history of diabetes?"

"None." Alaistair was well aware that what had happened to Richard could be due to any number of things. But he was in no position to discover them now in extremis. Judythe had also said that he hadn't choked on anything before becoming unconscious.

As Olivier stood there watching miserably, Gabrielle stared at the scene feeling helpless, and Judythe knelt beside Richard, sobbing quietly, the ten-man team of the SAMU appeared in the hallway, led by Yvonne. They were carrying a mountain of rescue equipment. They spoke to Alaistair and assessed the situation. They applied their own defibrillator, which worked only briefly, and they worked on him right where he lay, with the door to their room wide open, and Richard naked. One of the SAMU team covered his body with a drape. Guests had begun to come out of their rooms by then, from the noise of the medical team, and were alarmed at what they saw. The SAMU team put up a privacy screen around him, and Olivier tried to reassure the guests and urged them to go back in their rooms. Many were loath to, and wanted to see what was happening, as Yvonne hurried downstairs to the front desk.

"Why don't they pull him into their room and close the door?" Gabrielle asked Alaistair as he stepped away from the heat of the action, and allowed the French medics to do their work.

"It's a philosophy," he explained to her. "They work on the patient where they find him, without moving him or her, until the patient is stabilized. I know the Americans rush them to the hospital. In France, they treat cases like this where they occur. They don't want to waste time moving them, or risk making them worse."

"Do you think he'll be okay?" she asked in a whisper, and when he gazed at her, his eyes were bleak.

"It's possible. I don't know. I've seen worse cases when the victims survived, and other cases when they didn't," he said in a low voice. "It's likely to be a previously undiagnosed problem with his heart."

"I think they're on their honeymoon. I saw them when they checked in. They were so sweet." They could still hear Judythe crying behind the screen, and the urgent exchanges of the medical team. Gabrielle didn't want to intrude, but she didn't want to just close her door and abandon them either. The British doctor from across the hall had been very helpful. "What sort of doctor are you?" she asked him in an undervoice, as the team continued to work on

Richard, and they stood a few feet away. The hallway seemed jammed with people and action with the SAMU there. The SAMU team was totally blocking the hallway and access to the elevators, and the other guests just had to live with it. They wouldn't allow anyone to pass and interrupt their work, while they attempted to save Richard. They had gotten his heart started several times, and it failed again each time.

"I'm a lowly internist," he said modestly, but he looked concerned and intelligent. He had been very kind to Judythe, and had rapidly taken charge of the scene when he told Judythe to call the SAMU and Gabrielle to go downstairs to tell the hotel. "He's young, which should help," but they both knew that it didn't always. "It may be some kind of undetected congenital anomaly that he's lived with all his life, and it finally surfaced. That happens," but not always with happy results, he knew.

"I hope he'll be all right," Gabrielle said softly, waiting with him for news in the doorway of his room. She didn't want to leave the scene, nor did he. Her door was standing open, a little farther down the hall, past where the SAMU were working on Richard behind the screen. "They're so young. They deserve to be happy," Gabrielle said sadly.

"We all do," he said with a wintry smile.

But how many of us really were, Gabrielle wondered. She'd been happy with Arthur too, a long time ago now. Things started out right, and then they got complicated.

After an hour and a half, spread out in the doorway to Richard and Judythe's room, and pouring out into the hallway, the SAMU team continued to work on him, administering IVs, the defibrillator, chest compressions, giving him injections. Keeping him alive was a complex process, but he wasn't dead yet. A cardiologist had appeared on the scene after the first few minutes. He had come separately, and was directing the others and had taken charge.

Olivier was still in the hallway and tried to convince Gabrielle and Alaistair to go back to their respective rooms. The SAMU said that they didn't want to leave until they knew what was happening, in case Judythe needed them, particularly since she didn't speak French. Alaistair had translated for her and the SAMU several times, and assured them that he would handle whatever was necessary. But Alaistair and Gabrielle felt tied to the scene now, and invested in its outcome. Richard still hadn't regained consciousness, but the SAMU hadn't given up yet. Alaistair and Gabrielle stood together at the door to his room, quietly watching the scene, and he occasionally explained to her what was happening, and what procedures they were probably implementing. At one point, Yvonne came back upstairs to check on the scene herself and tell Olivier that the phones were working again. That seemed much less important now. Olivier was panicked that a guest was going to die during their first week back in operation. The owners wouldn't be happy about it, and if he died in the room, they would have to quarantine the room for forty days, which wasn't good news either. At least it wasn't one of the big suites, he whispered to Yvonne, and she gave him a dark look. He was perspiring and nervous and periodically guests stuck their heads out of their rooms to see if the drama had been resolved.

* * *

Patrick had heard the voices shouting from his own room since the commotion started. He had peeked out through the door after opening it a crack, and when he saw the hallway bustling with people and rescue equipment, he closed the door soundlessly and knew he'd have to wait. The blood from Sergei's head had crossed the marble and seeped into one of the carpets by then, and the fact that he was lying there naked seemed somehow obscene. Every time Patrick looked at him, he started crying again, not for the death of such an evil person, but for what it would mean for him now. The damage would be immeasurable.

He had thought of a dozen different versions of the story he would tell, but above all, he had to get out of the hotel and as far away as he could, before Sergei's body was discovered. He had never intended for this to happen, although admittedly his death would mean freedom from the blackmail and even his own addiction to him. Sergei wasn't the first man he had met in a hotel room somewhere, but it was the first time he had stayed involved for so long, had become hopelessly addicted to a sexual partner and in his thrall. It was the first time he'd ever been blackmailed, and certainly the first time he had been involved in a man's death, even accidentally. It had been an accident, but who would believe that if they found out sex and blackmail were involved? What if the police thought he had pushed Sergei violently to his death?

Patrick was fully dressed by then, and he was careful not to walk in any of the areas where there was blood, so he didn't leave bloody footprints when he left. When they discovered Sergei, and would come to question Patrick, he was intending to say it must have happened after he left. Perhaps he could say he was mentoring him, but that didn't sound likely, even to him. He had no idea what he would say, but it couldn't be the truth, and he couldn't admit how well or how long he had known him, or that he was being blackmailed, or he would become a prime suspect.

It was an hour and a half before the voices seemed to be dying down in the hall. He looked again, and saw that the medical team was leaving. They had Richard on a gurney, and were heading toward the elevators, away from Patrick's room. This was going to be his best opportunity, when everyone was distracted and looking in the opposite direction. He had taken all his belongings, and had checked that he had left nothing in the room. He was carrying both of his small bags, and had retrieved the money. He left the Do Not Disturb light on, and slipped quietly out of the room, leaving Sergei to be found later.

Without a sound, Patrick slipped down a service stairway, emerged on the main floor, and found his way to the lobby. No one paid any attention when he left, or seemed to recognize him. He walked swiftly down the Faubourg to a taxi stand, and got in the first cab. He gave his home address and said nothing more. The African driver didn't recognize him. Patrick paid him and got out, and let himself into his house. His wife, Alice, was out, his daughter, Marina, was at university in Lille, and his son, Damien, had recently gotten his own apartment, so no one saw him come home. He put the money in his desk drawer and locked it, and sat in the dark in his study, tears sliding down his face, terrified of what would come next. He had everything to lose if the police figured out the truth. Only lies could save him now. The death of the young Russian dancer meant nothing to him. Patrick was the victim, in his mind, not Sergei. Patrick had so much to lose. And Sergei was an opportunistic lowlife who had preyed on him. Patrick felt nothing for him now.

Richard was in an ambulance leaving the hotel by then with Judythe beside him. His heart was beating, but he was still unconscious. He had never regained consciousness. The cardiac team was waiting for him at the Pitié Salpêtrière, one of the largest, most efficient hospitals in Paris. Judythe had promised to let Gabrielle and Alaistair know what had happened when they got there. She had been assured by the SAMU that there would be doctors at the hospital who spoke English, and neither Gabrielle nor Alaistair wanted to intrude on two people who were essentially strangers, although they felt sorry for both of them. Judythe looked frantic and pale when they left.

The other guests were able to leave their rooms then, with the medical team gone, and Alaistair looked at Gabrielle, shaken. They both were.

"Do you want to go downstairs to the bar for a drink?" he suggested kindly. He and Gabrielle had both stood by steadfastly while the scene played out.

"I think I'd faint if I did. Do you want to come to my room?" she offered. Neither of them wanted to be alone after what they'd seen. It had been rugged, and a very close call for Richard. He wasn't out of the woods yet, and was barely stable, according to the doctors. He was just stable enough to move him now and for further intervention at the hospital.

Alaistair followed Gabrielle into her enormous suite, and admired it. They introduced themselves and sat down. At her suggestion, Alaistair poured himself a drink, and Gabrielle ordered tea from room service. They talked about what had happened, and she told him she'd come to Paris to attend the Biennale, when he asked why she was there. She explained that she was an art consultant, advised people on their art purchases, and helped them acquire what they needed or wanted to expand their collections.

"This used to be my favorite hotel," she said. "I've missed it. So, I decided to stay here when they reopened."

"It's my first time," he said, smiling. "It's incredibly beautiful and comfortable, other than the incident tonight. And they don't seem to have the bugs out of their phone system yet. I thought I'd give myself a treat and stay here before a meeting tomorrow."

Her tea arrived, and they spent a pleasant hour together chatting, slowly calming down, when Alaistair stood up and said he thought he'd go to the hospital and see how Judythe was faring, and if she needed any help talking to the doctors. Gabrielle thought it was a kind gesture. He had just left a few minutes earlier when she heard a bloodcurdling scream from down the hallway and then silence. The Louis XVI wasn't peaceful anymore. Her nerves were still jangled after the dramatic scene with the SAMU. It felt like a TV show, not the peaceful hotel she knew. She wondered if the old manager would have handled the situation better. The new one had seemed overwhelmed.

In his office, Olivier was sheet white, and looked like he'd seen a ghost, after he got the call from the head housekeeper to give him the shocking news. A new night maid had gone into Patrick Martin's suite to offer turndown service and extra towels, disregarding the Do Not Disturb light that was on, and she had found a dead man lying naked in a pool of blood. The police had been called. They were about to arrive, and Olivier could envision his career going straight down the tubes. He didn't know who the dead man was, or how it happened, or even if it was Patrick Martin who was dead, which would be unimaginably awful for the hotel's reputation. He was about to find out. They had been told by the police not to enter the room or touch anything. It was a crime scene now.

Gabrielle saw the police arrive from her window, hordes of them, and she heard them going down the hall past her room. They filled the hallway, including a SWAT team, and when she peeked out of her room, she saw that several of them had their guns drawn, not knowing what they'd find. She didn't know what had happened. But one thing was for sure. With that many police involved, it couldn't be anything good. Her mind raced to the possibility of some kind of terrorist attack that was taking place, or had occurred in the hotel. She double locked the door to her room, and prayed that she was safe there.

The phones were working again, and Gabrielle and all the guests on the third floor received a call from Yvonne Philippe at the front desk. She explained that there was a "minor problem" on the third floor. The police were arriving on the scene to handle it and the guests were not in danger. But they were asking the guests not to leave their rooms for the moment, until the police gave them the all clear.

Yvonne was quick to tell all the third floor guests that for the inconvenience of the SAMU in the hall earlier, and now this incident, they would not be charged for their hotel accommodations for that night, with the sincere apologies of the management for any inconvenience. It had been Yvonne's idea to offer them a free night. Olivier was grateful, as he saw the police arrive, fill the lobby, and rush up the stairs to the third floor, as the guests in the lobby stared in amazement. It was an unfamiliar and alarming sight at the Louis XVI. They had no idea what had occurred or what would happen next. The reopening of the hotel was off to a very bumpy start.

Chapter 4

Alaistair had left the hotel minutes before the maid's piercing scream echoed through the third floor hall. He was in a cab on the way to the hospital where Richard had been taken. He wanted to reassure himself that Richard was still alive and, if it seemed appropriate, to offer his help to Judythe, if she needed someone with her for support. She was far from home, didn't speak the language, and had been frightened when she left in the ambulance with Richard still unconscious, but at least alive. Alaistair didn't want to be intrusive, but helpful to her, since he was a doctor.

When he reached the Pitié Salpêtrière, he inquired about Richard. He was told at the main desk that he was currently being worked on by their cardiac trauma team, and they explained where to find the patient's wife. He followed the labyrinthian halls of the hospital to the location he'd been given, and found Judythe sitting in a waiting area, white-faced and frightened. She looked up gratefully when she saw him. Alaistair was a tall man with a young face, silver hair, and kind blue eyes. He slid quietly into a chair next to her, and she tried to smile as tears rolled down her face.

"Any news?" he asked softly, and she shook her head.

"Thank you for saving him," she said in a choked voice.

"You did as much as I did," he reminded her. "You would have been fine without me. The SAMU does a good job here, and this is an excellent hospital. French hospitals aren't much for creature comforts," and it looked that way to her too. The hospital was gloomy with none of the warmer touches she was used to in American hospitals. "But they're medically excellent, and this is one of the best in Paris, possibly in Europe. He's in good hands," Alaistair reassured her, and he looked hesitant for a moment. "I thought I'd see if they'd tell me anything I could pass on to you. Would you like me to stay, or would that be an imposition?" He was very polite and respectful. She quickly touched his arm, and he saw that her hand was shaking.

"Would you mind staying? The doctor taking care of him speaks English, but I'm too scared to understand half of what they're saying. They want to do a bunch of scans and tests. They said we kept his oxygen levels high enough while he was unconscious, but they don't know what caused it. We've both been under a lot of stress for the last year. We've both just gotten divorced, and his was particularly nasty."

"Mrs. Gates, the guest at the hotel, and I thought that you might be on your honeymoon. You're both so young." He was careful to keep it in the present tense, and Judythe smiled and nodded.

"It's not our honeymoon yet. His divorce just came through a few weeks ago. It's final now. We're going to get married very soon, or . . . we were . . ." She choked on a sob and looked at Alaistair sadly. "We met at my wedding two years ago. He was a college room-mate of my ex-husband's and things just happened. We tried to resist it at first, but we couldn't. So, we both got divorced. We were finally free, and now this." She squeezed her eyes shut as tears slid freely down her cheeks, and he patted her hand.

"Things like this happen in life. It gets complicated. When they figure out the problem with his heart, and why it happened, more than likely they'll be able to fix it, and you'll go on from here to share your lives together. You saved his life today." The brutal irony that he could die now, on the brink of starting their new life together, wasn't lost on him, or on her.

"Maybe this is our punishment for destroying two marriages, and hurting the people we were married to."

"I don't believe in that, and those marriages can't have been very solid if you and Richard fell in love, and were so willing to fight for the future you envisioned together."

"We shouldn't have married the people we did. At thirty-seven, I was afraid I'd never find the right person, so I married the wrong one so I could have children. And Richard said he always knew that his was wrong too. She was the right person on paper, but not in real life."

"At least there are no children involved, and you can go on from here." He did not add "if he lives," but they both thought it.

He brought Judythe a cup of coffee from a machine, while they waited, and it was a full two hours before the doctor in charge of Richard's case came to find them in the waiting room. Richard was still unconscious, but the doctor said that all the necessary scans had been performed. The doctor's English was fluent, with a heavy accent, but he was easy to understand.

"We will need to do surgery on your husband," he said to Judythe, since she had claimed to be his wife. "We know where the problem lies, but we need to see more closely the extent of the damage. We believe it is a congenital anomaly that could have declared itself at any time, as a boy or later. It's unusual that it took so long to expose itself. In most cases, if we are right about our assessment, it is the kind of anomaly which causes a seemingly healthy twenty-year-old to die while playing sports, or in the shower at twenty-five. He is fortunate that he survived it, thanks to both of you, if I understand the role you both played before the SAMU arrived."

"Is the surgery very dangerous?" Judythe asked him. She had been told that he was a professor as well as a cardiac surgeon, apparently a notable one.

"There is no choice. What he has and what happened to him is very dangerous. He will not survive without the surgery. We believe that he has an ineffective valve in his heart, which held out much longer than normal in these cases. If we can, we will replace it, and hope it won't trouble him again. We also need to determine if this episode damaged his heart irreparably. We cannot tell without the surgery. We will be a team of three surgeons consulting and operating on him, with a full support team. It's a delicate surgery, and an important one. If we are successful, this event will have been a blessing for him. The valve could have failed at a time and place where he couldn't be saved, so the circumstances are optimal to do the valve replacement, if it's possible." Judythe nodded. "It will be an open-heart procedure, and he could lose a considerable amount of blood, but we are prepared for that possibility. We have done procedures like this many times. He's still a young man, he's strong, and he appears to be in good health otherwise. I believe that his chances are good. We need to replace the damaged valve as soon as possible, if he is to make a full recovery. If not, we will have to consider alternate strategies. We are hoping for the least amount of damage and consequences for the future."

"When will you do it?" she asked, trying to process everything he had told her. The doctor had been very clear.

"In an hour, if you give us the permission, Mrs. Sheffield. I am waiting for one of my colleagues to arrive. We have already consulted him, and he agrees with our assessment. The other surgeon is already here and examined your husband with me." It occurred to Judythe that she had no right to sign the permission for the surgery. But Richard had no living parents, and no siblings, so she was the closest he had to next of kin. It was an awesome responsibility, and there seemed to be no other choice than to risk the surgery. The surgeon spelled it out for her again as she hesitated. "If we do not attempt to replace the defective valve, he won't survive."

"You have my permission," she said in a barely audible voice, and the doctor thanked her, and said that the nurse would bring her the appropriate papers to sign. He was cool and professional, and everything about him inspired confidence in his abilities. She turned to Alaistair after the doctor walked away. "Do you agree with him?" she asked anxiously.

"Yes, I do," Alaistair answered quietly, as they sat down again. They had stood to speak to the doctor. The surgeon appeared to be in his early fifties, a few years older than Richard. "I'm an internist, not a cardiac surgeon, so he knows what's needed far better than I do. But it sounds like Richard has a good chance with the surgery, and none without it. I don't think you have much choice here, Judythe. The worst has already happened. This isn't an optional surgery now, it's a vital necessity to save his life, and give him some kind of a future." It was how she had read the situation too.

The nurse arrived with the papers a few minutes later, and Judythe signed them with a shaking hand. She signed her own last name, "Oakes," and no one questioned the difference of last names. She felt as though she was signing his life away, and she asked the nurse if she could see him before the surgery. Her English was not as good as the surgeon's, Alaistair translated her request, and the nurse responded that they were already preparing him for surgery but Judythe could see him for a few minutes. She explained that he was on a respirator, and was now in a medically induced coma, and would be after the surgery as well.

She left and returned a few minutes later to take Judythe down a series of confusing back halls to a pre-surgical prep room, where several nurses were monitoring the various machines Richard was hooked up to. Seeing him took her breath away for a moment. She stood close to him, and gently touched his hand. He was hooked up to IVs, and there were various mechanical sounds and beeps and lights from the machines and monitors. The head anesthesiologist came into the room and nodded to her, and with a last look at Richard, she followed the nurse out of the room. She felt like her own heart was in a vise, remembering that only hours before they had been strolling in the Tuileries Gardens, laughing and talking about their future, feeling lucky, and they had made love right before his heart failed. She felt guilty, wondering if that had caused it.

She went back to the waiting room where Alaistair was still waiting for her. He watched her approach. She was a beautiful, blond woman, with the tall, clean healthy looks that some American women have. She and Richard made a handsome couple. She was still wearing the clothes she had thrown on hastily when she left in the ambulance with Richard. She sat down heavily next to Alaistair. Richard didn't even look like himself, attached to all the monitors, and with the respirator tube in his mouth, while the machine breathed for him. She was relieved to have Alaistair with her although they were naturally strangers. It would have been even more frightening alone.

The surgeon had told her that the surgery would take from five to seven hours. Alaistair offered to take her out for something to eat. It was almost ten o'clock by then, and she hadn't eaten, but she couldn't have.

"No, but thank you. You should go back to the hotel. I'll be fine." One of the nurses had brought her a pillow and a blanket, and she was planning to spend the night there. She wanted to be near him in case anything happened. She would have gone mad waiting in their room at the hotel. She wanted to be here, as close to him as she could be. "You don't need to stay," she reassured Alaistair, grateful for the time he had spent with her. He had been inordinately kind to perfect strangers. He looked almost as tired as Judythe did.

"I have a rather important meeting tomorrow morning, or I'd offer to stay here with you tonight." He couldn't think of anything sadder than her being alone in a foreign hospital, not sure if her loved one would live or die, or if their future would end that night, after they'd fought so hard for it. Life was cruel at times. The surgeon said that they felt they had about a thirty percent chance for a successful outcome, which was both encouraging and terrifying, depending on how you looked at it. The battle was by no means won yet, and Judythe was fully cognizant of that when she thanked Alaistair again, and he left, after giving her his cellphone number, if she needed it, and promising to call her the next day after his meeting. He had told her to contact him at any hour, if she needed his help. But there wasn't much he could do.

He walked for a little while after leaving the hospital, thinking about Judythe and Richard, and the future they had fought for, and their trip to Paris to celebrate their future, which might end in tragedy that night. Their lives had taken a turn that no one could have predicted. Suddenly their chosen path had veered sharply and changed direction toward a very dark place.

Alaistair took a cab back to the hotel, and texted Gabrielle about Richard's surgery from the taxi. At least he was still alive and had a chance. They could already have been mourning him if the SAMU hadn't arrived and interceded in time.

He was startled to see several police cars and vans outside the hotel, a SWAT team standing by with their automatic weapons, and more police in the lobby. He wondered what had happened in his absence for the past few hours, if there had been a terrorist threat or some kind of attack. No one questioned him or stopped him when he crossed the lobby to the elevator, and when he got to the third floor, there were more police clustered in the hallway. He quietly slipped into his room, and lay down on the bed. He was exhausted after his part in the drama around Richard. It had been a trying night, and his plans to have a good dinner on his own in Paris were long forgotten. He was worried about his meeting the next day, but he could already guess how that would turn out. He had very little hope about it, but was going to go to the meeting anyway. It was a good excuse for coming to Paris, although the trip so far was not what he had expected. Alaistair knew better than anyone that life was like that and how quickly everything could change and go wrong.

The night so far had been incredibly stressful for Olivier Bateau. His assistant, Yvonne, had been helpful, dealing with both the police and the guests, but the responsibility rested on him. A grisly murder on the premises, involving an important man, was every hotel manager's worst nightmare. The victim's clothes and identification papers were in the suite. The police had run him through their computers. He was a twenty-seven-year-old Russian citizen, had come to France as a ballet dancer with a Russian troupe, and was currently a model, with no particular success. There were 140 euros in his wallet, and he was wearing an expensive watch, so robbery was clearly not the motive. Cause of death had been the impact to his skull when he fell to the marble floor. There were no other signs of violence in the room, no furniture overturned, no marks on his body, no stab wounds or evidence of gunshot wounds. They did not know if he had fallen or been pushed.

There was a small stool near the body, but it wasn't overturned. He was naked, with his clothes in a heap in the bathroom, a hotel robe cast aside that had been worn, and evidence of sexual acts in the bed. There was no sign of the minister of the interior in the room, but he was the guest who had checked in, and there was nothing to link him to the dead man, except that he had died in Patrick Martin's room. No maid had seen them together, the only maid who had seen Sergei was the one who had mistakenly disregarded the Do Not Disturb light and had entered the room and found the body. When the police checked, an order had been placed with room service for foie gras, caviar, and vodka.

A single glass stood next to the vodka bottle, and another with remnants of scotch stood on the coffee table. They hadn't been checked for prints or DNA yet. The room service waiter who had taken the order was unable to say who had placed the order, or if he had a Russian accent, since the waiter himself was Italian, and didn't speak French well enough to determine if the caller was Russian or French. The waiter who had delivered the order had seen only one man, in a hotel bathrobe, who had signed for it, but he didn't know who the man was and there was no evidence to indicate whether the order was for one person or two. But according to the waiter, no second person appeared to be present in the room. They showed him a press photograph of Patrick Martin and the waiter didn't recognize him, but he said he wasn't sure. He said he hadn't looked closely at the man who'd signed the room service check.

The police were at a loss to determine if it was an accidental death from a fall, or if, worst case, it was homicide. The setting, the look and age of the victim, and the sexual evidence in the bed pointed to the probability that it was a sexual encounter, but they couldn't be sure yet if it involved Patrick Martin, or a third party who had met the Russian there after Martin left.

The sheets had been taken by the police as evidence for DNA tests.

Complications

None of the hotel staff had noticed anything unusual. They hadn't questioned the hotel guests yet, although they would eventually, but the hotel manager had begged them not to, and it didn't seem as though they would know anything more than anyone else. And to complicate matters further, their technical bugs had caused the security cameras to go black for three hours on the first five floors. By midnight, it was clear that the key person they had to interview was the minister of the interior himself, since he had reserved the room. Jacques Forrestier, the chief detective in charge of the investigation, commented on the opulence of the suite, and the manager had said that the reservation request was for a basic room, and they had upgraded him. Olivier Bateau said Patrick Martin had told the manager that he planned to use the room for a meeting, and had been unhappy to be given a grand suite, and wanted to be downgraded again, but they'd had no simple rooms to give him. He wasn't charged for the luxurious suite, but only for a standard room, per his request.

The chief detective thought there was possibly a reasonable explanation for the minister's involvement, and hoped it wasn't of a sexual nature, which would inevitably lead to scandal, but there were numerous more benign possibilities, which would have involved a third party they knew nothing about, and Patrick Martin might not either. It didn't look good for the moment, but it wasn't a political disaster yet, and he hoped it wouldn't be. Martin was a respectable man with a clean reputation, and a family, and the last thing the detective wanted, and the government needed, was a scandal on their hands, involving murder and a government minister. His assistant, Detective Michel Plante, was less optimistic than he was.

"You know yourself, if it smells rotten, and looks rotten, it probably is rotten. And a situation as potentially rotten as this one doesn't usually turn out to smell like a rose."

"Martin is fifty-four years old, and he's never been involved in a scandal before," his chief reminded him. "I don't think he's that kind of guy. He's all about family, and critical of all our presidents who had mistresses and illegitimate children, and politicians who turn out to be gay, having sex with little boys." And they already knew by then that the victim was no innocent. He had been arrested for soliciting, and lewd homosexual acts in a public space. The modeling agency where he worked had supplied the information that he was a gold digger, hoping to latch on to a rich patron to support him, which was supposedly why he had come to Paris. They didn't seem to like him much, and said he was arrogant.

"Maybe he was blackmailing Patrick Martin," the assistant suggested, and the chief shook his head.

"I'd put my hand in the fire on this one that there isn't a chance in hell of that. Martin is too clean and too smart to set himself up for blackmail."

"All the more reason for Martin to be vulnerable to blackmail, if there's a dark secret there. You know as well as I do, anything is possible. The clean ones always have the worst secrets. Politics is a dirty business."

By midnight, they had gleaned all they could from the hotel employees on duty, and despite the late hour, the chief detective felt that it was vitally important that they speak to Patrick Martin that night to hear what he had to say about whether or not there was a simple explanation to account for the presence of a dead man in the hotel room he had taken at the Louis XVI. If there was a sensible explanation for it, Forrestier wanted to know before the press got hold of the story. With a dead male model in one of Paris's fanciest hotels, in a room taken by the minister of the interior, the media would find it, and have a heyday with it. Forrestier just hoped there was an explanation they could all live with.

After the two detectives left the hotel, they headed toward Patrick Martin's address in the sixteenth arrondissement. Some people from the police crime lab were going to go over the room meticulously the next day, looking for further evidence. The room would be quarantined for the next forty days anyway, due to the death there, much to the manager's dismay. Losing that kind of income was a circumstance all hotel managers dreaded, particularly when they lost the use of very expensive suites. Hotels often went to great lengths to avoid losing a suite to quarantine, even sometimes hiring unscrupulous doctors who would put an IV in the arm of a person who had just died in their hotel room, claiming they were still alive, and then saying that death occurred in the ambulance or once they reached the hospital. But in this case, there was no question about the Russian model's death. The evidence of it was in a pool of blood on the white marble floor of the room. Bateau was wondering now too whether the white marble floor the man had died on would be irreparably stained and have to be replaced. It was the least of their problems, but the owners would be upset about that too, particularly since the delivery time for fine Italian marble could take up to a year, even longer than the police quarantine.

The main question now for the police to find out was if foul play was involved. If so, the case was going to blow wide open. And if not, Patrick Martin was home free.

* * *

The house was dark and silent when Patrick got home that night, with every fiber of his being reverberating after what had happened with Sergei. He had locked the money in his desk, and sat for an hour in his darkened study, shaking and trying to work out the best story to tell the police. He knew they would inevitably question him since he had booked the room.

He was going to tell them that he had met briefly with Sergei. The meeting had been uneventful. He didn't dare claim that he had also met with someone else. Perhaps he could say that Sergei was giving him information on someone and acting as an informant about a fellow Russian, laundering money, which was common and highly illegal, and a credible story. He could say that Sergei was afraid of being seen so Martin had booked the room. He would then say that he had left the hotel a short time later, at the conclusion of the meeting. Sergei had been unable to supply the proof they needed, but had promised to deliver it soon. Patrick left then and went home, but before he left the hotel, Sergei had asked if Patrick minded if he stayed in the room for a little longer. Everything that had happened after that, which led to Sergei being found dead in a pool of his own blood, must have occurred after Patrick had left, with a third person Patrick had never laid eyes on, possibly or even probably coming to the suite to meet Sergei.

It was the cleanest story Patrick could think of, and seemed to serve the purpose. He was worried about the cameras in the hotel, but they had been beeping with flashing light signals when he left, and Patrick was praying that they might have malfunctioned as well as the phones. If not, he'd have to explain leaving by the service stairs, but he could blame the SAMU for that, since they had blocked the path to the elevator for at least two hours.

It would still look questionable in the press, but an accidental death in the course of a money-laundering case against a mysterious Russian might serve the purpose. A male model found dead in a very fancy hotel room that Patrick Martin had booked looked unsavory, but hopefully they could skate past that, if the police believed him, and no one would be the wiser. He tried to compose himself, and he had another scotch, straight up, when he got home. His wife, Alice, went to a monthly women's dinner with her girlfriends and was with them that night, which was why he had chosen that evening to meet Sergei.

He and Alice had not had an easy marriage. He had been a young lawyer when they married, and had intended to pursue a career in business or law. She became a professor of French literature at the Sorbonne, and was the classic bourgeois wife, from a respectable family. He had thought she was the right choice for his career, but she proved to be a lackluster wife and constantly complained. When he was offered an opportunity in the Ministry of the Interior, he was sorely tempted. It sounded exciting to him, with numerous perks, none of which appealed to Alice. He took the job anyway, and she had been unhappy ever since. She had continued teaching at the Sorbonne and their lives had become increasingly separate over the years. They had nothing in common, and their marriage was a habit neither of them had the courage to break, and it looked better for his job if he was married.

Their two children, Marina and Damien, were born during the early days of his career. He worked long hours on matters he couldn't discuss with Alice and he hardly saw his children. But in time his family gave him the perfect cover for the secret life he had only dreamed of, and eventually began to indulge in. Alice and his children never knew. No one he knew did. At first his sexual encounters with men were occasional, but the desire became insatiable. He had a raw hunger and need for young men, like a vampire in need of blood, and whenever a willing young beautiful man crossed his path, he would arrange to meet him in secret for violent, passionate sex. They weren't romantic liaisons, they were purely carnal and exciting, and they allowed him to continue his deadly boring life with Alice. He hadn't loved her in years, if ever. He doubted now if he had ever loved her. He had known by the time the children were born that he had made a terrible mistake, but he could live with it, as long as he had his clandestine encounters, which were all the more exciting because they were forbidden.

It had never backfired or gotten out of hand until he met Sergei, who was ambitious, greedy, and had a criminal nature. None of the young men Patrick met with ever knew who he was. The anonymity contributed to the excitement and heightened the passion for him. Sergei knew who he was. He recognized him at the gay bar where they met, but Patrick risked it anyway. After the second time he met him, Sergei began to blackmail him. And by then it was too late. Sergei had his hooks into him and Patrick was addicted to him, like a drug. It had gone on for two years now. Sergei constantly upped the ante, as he had tried to do that night. Patrick could no longer keep up with Sergei's demands, but politically he could not afford not to. He had too much at stake now. The Russian knew it, and took full advantage of him. It had reached breaking point for Patrick. He could no longer afford to keep siphoning money out of the joint account he had with Alice. At first, it had been easy to explain, but there was no possible explanation for the amounts Sergei had wanted recently. The more powerful Patrick was becoming politically, the more money Sergei demanded.

Patrick knew that Alice had been bored with him for years, and disappointed in her life with him. Other people were impressed by his title and power. She wasn't. She hated his job, and they had an aversion to each other. He knew she only stayed married to him because she was a respectable woman and didn't want to get divorced. Being married to him was the lesser of two evils, and she said she did it for the children. She would have preferred having a husband who was head of a bank, or a businessman. As minister of the interior, she thought of him as a sleazy politician, or a policeman by a fancier name. Their sex life had ended years before. She suspected him of cheating on her occasionally, but never made an issue of it, since he appeared respectable. Never in a million years would she have guessed that men were his passion. In fact, he always made a point with his family and among close friends of being outspoken against gay men. His intimates accused him of being homophobic.

He had known his preference when he married Alice, but thought he could keep it in control with rare encounters. In fact, he couldn't and his appetite for men had grown over the years. He needed a male body next to him to feel alive and powerful. He liked the dangerous ones, like Sergei, not the tame ones. And now, look where it had led him, and what would he say to Alice? The same as to the police. He respected her as the mother of his children, but he hadn't touched her in years and knew he never would again. All he wanted now was to get through this. He rehearsed the story over and over in his head, and tried to forget the image of Sergei lying dead in his own blood at the Louis XVI.

He was slightly drunk when Alice came home from her women's dinner that night. She heard him in his study, but didn't stop by to say hello. It was late. She was tired. She'd had a good time with her women friends and didn't want to spoil it with the icy, unfriendly exchanges she usually had with Patrick. Sometimes she thought he hated her, and most of the time she thought he didn't even care that much. They had been strangers under the same roof for so long that it seemed normal to them. She had no interest in his career, and he had none in hers. He thought her life as a French literature professor was intensely boring. They only warmed up a little when the children were around, and on rare occasions shared family evenings. But their children had their own lives now. Marina was following in her mother's footsteps, studying English literature, with an eye to teaching later on, and Damien worked in PR, in a firm that handled luxury fashion brands. He hoped to own his own PR firm one day.

Alice's only value to Patrick now was for his political career. If he succeeded in winning the election this time or the next, she would be the perfect first lady for the president of France. He never lost sight of that, nor did she. She knew it was what kept him with her, and she could live without the rest. She had her children, her friends, and her work at the Sorbonne, which she still found rewarding. She had given up any thought of romance in her life a long time ago. She was an honest, decent woman, and would never have done anything to put his career at risk. She was fifty-two years old, not sexy or beautiful, but she had a quiet, distinguished style about her that the public would respect. She was the perfect accessory for his political life. She knew that as long as his political ambitions burned within him, he would never leave her. And even though she had hated his career until then, she rather liked the idea of becoming first lady of France. It somehow made the long years of an unhappy marriage seem worthwhile, and a suitable reward for the loveless years she had spent with him. She knew he didn't love her, and she accepted it so as not to live with the shame of a divorce. No one in her family had ever gotten divorced.

Patrick was still in his study when the police arrived at his home at one A.M. Alice was awake too, and surprised to hear the buzzer from downstairs. She glanced out the window and saw a police car outside, at the curb. She assumed he must be involved in an important case, concerning some major criminal. Patrick could guess what it was about, drained his glass of scotch, and buzzed them in.

He greeted Detective Forrestier and Detective Plante with a surprised expression, still wearing his suit and tie, and let them into his apartment.

"Is there an emergency, gentlemen?" He smiled pleasantly. Both detectives maintained their sober expression.

"You may think so, Minister. Could we speak to you in private?"

He led them to his study, and followed them in. He closed the door behind him and indicated two chairs across from his desk, as he sat down and looked at them. "It's late, so it must be important. What can I do to assist you? I assume it couldn't wait until the morning or you wouldn't be here." He spoke calmly, and appeared unconcerned, the last scotch had helped steady his nerves.

"No, it couldn't wait," Detective Forrestier confirmed. He cut to the chase as Patrick waited expectantly. "It's about Sergei Karpov, a young Russian model." Nothing in Patrick's expression indicated whether he knew him or not. He wanted to know what they knew before he said anything. "I assume you knew him. He was found dead in a hotel suite at the Hotel Louis XVI tonight, a suite registered in your name. We are investigating whether there was foul play involved or not. We'd like you to enlighten us about your involvement with him." Forrestier was playing the same game as Patrick. The two men locked their eyes on each other across Patrick's desk. They were like two panthers circling each other, poised to strike if necessary, taking the measure of their opponent, waiting to know more, and determining which of them would win. Patrick was willing to fight to the death. Everything he cared about was at stake. All he had to do was come out of it unscathed, and whatever it took, he intended to do that. With Sergei conveniently dead now, he thought he had a chance.

Chapter 5

T he two police detectives spent an hour with Patrick that night, in the privacy of his study. He had played the scenario over so many times in his mind before they came that his performance was almost flawless, as he went over what had happened with them.

Patrick explained to them in a slightly supercilious way that the government had been pursuing an important Russian, from the underworld, for nearly two years now, on a highly confidential case few were aware of. They were seeking to prosecute him for money laundering and tax evasion, and vast amounts of money were involved. They were hoping to seize his many properties in France. Patrick informed them that the case was too sensitive to share the name of the subject yet, but Sergei had become an informant for them, and had contact with the subject of the investigation. He was supplying them with information that could ultimately lead to the man's arrest.

"Were you paying him for the information, Minister?" Detective Forrestier asked.

"Sometimes," Patrick said vaguely, and didn't disclose the amounts.

"And you were handling the case yourself?"

"I met with the victim a few times myself. He said he had fresh information for us, but wanted to meet in a secure location where no one in the subject's circle would see him. I suggested we meet at the Louis XVI, and booked a room for that purpose for tonight. I asked for a simple room, and was rather annoyed when they upgraded me to a much larger one, a suite." What he said had already been corroborated by the manager of the hotel, who had been startled by Patrick's displeasure at being given a much larger room, one of their best suites. "We met earlier this evening, in the room at the hotel. The meeting turned out to be disappointing, and in fact, he had no new information of significance to give us, but promised he would soon. I think he was hoping for another payment. The meeting didn't last long, and wasn't worth my time. I suggested he leave before me, but since it had taken less time than expected, he said he needed to stay out of sight for another hour or so, he asked if I would mind if he left the room after I did. I said it was fine. I left, not wanting to waste more time with him. He was very much alive when I left and came home. How was he killed? Was he shot? Did he shoot himself?" His mask of innocence seemed perfect. "Given the kind of people he consorted with, I can't say I'm entirely surprised that he died."

"The cause of death appears to have been a fall, backward onto a marble floor, fractured skull."

"And you think he was pushed?" Patrick was hungry for the answer to that question.

"We don't know yet. It's early in the investigation. But he was alive when you left?" the senior detective confirmed.

"Yes, he was. I'm afraid that's all I know. It was a futile meeting. Perhaps the reason he wanted to stay was to meet someone else there after I left, or show off to someone."

"It's a possibility, and we have no evidence of another visitor to the suite. Unfortunately, not all of the cameras were functioning. They seem to be having technical problems." The chief detective looked annoyed at that. Videotapes would have simplified everything.

"That's bad luck in this case." But very good luck for Patrick. He was relieved that his guess had been right and they were malfunctioning. He wondered what he might have overlooked, but couldn't think of anything. His fingerprints would be on the glass of scotch, but he admitted he was there. The detectives didn't seem skeptical about his story. It all made sense. "He consorted with some very dangerous people in his line of work. I'm not surprised he came to a bad end, as I said. But it's bad luck to lose an informant."

"It sounds like bad luck for all of us," Detective Forrestier said, looking tired. It had been a long night. "We're going to keep it from the media for another twenty-four hours if we can, to see what turns up."

"That seems wise," Patrick said, looking thoughtful. "I'm sorry not to have more information."

"Did you order any food while you were there?" Detective Plante asked him, to see what he would say.

"No, I didn't," Patrick said in a brave moment, feeling confident. It had gone well so far. "I suppose Karpov may have charged something to me after I left. Nothing too extravagant, I hope." Plante nodded, but didn't comment. He didn't remind him that he'd signed the check for room service. Patrick seemed to have forgotten. Or maybe he didn't want to admit to ordering extravagant items like foie gras and caviar. There was an open bottle of champagne, one of vodka, and scotch in a glass, a lot of alcohol for a short meeting between two men.

The two detectives left shortly afterward and Patrick went to his bedroom, and was surprised to see Alice still up. She glanced at him as she got into bed. They still shared a bedroom despite the cold relationship they shared. It looked better to the children.

"Why were the police here?" she asked him.

"Nothing important. An informant we've used was found dead." It all seemed unsavory to her, and she never asked about his work, nor did he about hers. They spoke of the children mostly when they had anything to say to each other. They weren't unique in that. They knew others whose marriages had lost their luster years before, and the children were the only bond they had between them now. It was enough, and in Patrick's case, his presidential aspirations were a bright shining star in their shared sky.

As far as he could tell, his meeting with the police had gone well. He hoped there wouldn't be another, and he had satisfied them adequately. It was just rotten luck that Sergei had fallen and died in a hotel room Patrick had booked in his own name. Ordinarily he used a false name and paid in cash when he met men in hotels. But he couldn't do that at the Louis XVI. But at least he was rid of Sergei now, and if nothing more came of it, then it had turned out well for him in the end. He wouldn't have to scrounge up the blackmail money anymore, and lie to his banker and his wife.

* * *

Alaistair woke at six the next morning, before his meeting with the professor whom his friend had referred him to. He didn't expect any earth-shattering revelations, but he was clinging to a thin thread of hope.

At nine o'clock sharp he was ushered into a barren, badly decorated office that looked more like a cheap motel with shabby furniture. The professor in question had an illustrious reputation, but was primarily a researcher now, and saw as few private patients as possible. He preferred research work for the greater good than demanding, unhappy, desperately ill patients who needed the kind of reassurance he had never been good at, and liked even less as he got older. He knew why Alaistair was coming to see him, and had offered little hope.

Alaistair only had to wait a few minutes until a nurse in a lab coat ushered him into the professor's office. His name was Jean-Claude Leblanc, and he had been doing research on acute lymphocytic leukemia, which Alaistair had been diagnosed with four months before. It had come as a shock at first, and the prognosis was devastating. The disease had progressed in silence, and was already in an advanced stage. He had been given six months to live, which meant, if they were right, he had two months left. Oddly, he didn't feel ill, just very tired, which was getting steadily worse. He was still practicing internal medicine, though working one day less for the past month. But the doctors had assured him that his not feeling very sick was deceptive, and the end would come quickly, with rapid deterioration in the final weeks. After careful consideration, he had refused all treatment, the protocols seeming worse than the disease until the end. He had seen too many of his friends and patients wither away from chemo and radiation, destroying their quality of life, until at the end death was a mercy. One was never quite sure if they died of the treatment or the illness. They had also recommended a bone marrow transplant. He refused to go that route, and if he slept what was left of his life away in the final weeks, or even now, what did it matter? He had no children, no wife. He had been divorced for years. He had had passing affairs for the last fifteen years, but never an important relationship.

He had made a decision within weeks of his diagnosis that when the end appeared to be near, or if he began to suffer, he would make a silent, dignified exit. It had been surprisingly easy to acquire the means to do so. He kept the pills with him, and brought them to Paris with him, in case the professor's verdict was too dire and he saw something even more ominous than Alaistair's doctors in London were seeing. He didn't intend to be taken by surprise. There was absolutely no doubt in Alaistair's mind about what he planned to do. He wasn't depressed about it. In fact, knowing that he had his escape route mapped out made him feel better about the entire situation. It was early to die, at forty-nine, but he had led a good life, and if he wasn't destined for more, then that was how the game had shaken out. He felt oddly peaceful about it now.

Professor Leblanc pronounced the same death sentence he had heard from his physicians in London, and outlined the same extreme treatment of chemotherapy and a bone marrow transplant, and possible immunotherapy to give him a few more months. He had pretended at first in London that he would go along with the treatment. He didn't bother to do that now in Paris.

"I've decided not to go that route," he said calmly, as the professor observed him.

"You can of course try experimental treatments, and there are some unusual ones out there, if you have access to them. But none of them have worked so far. Or you can decide to do absolutely nothing. You may buy a month or two with some of the experimental drugs, if that. But this form of leukemia is particularly tenacious, and moves quickly. I've done some work on it myself. You're welcome to try a format of treatment that I've been working on. I can't promise you a miracle with it. But I managed to stretch two months to a year for one of my patients, and six months to two years for another. That's something, I suppose, though not nearly effective enough. And one always hopes that during the additional time, some lucky researcher will come up with something else." He had been one of the early researchers on AIDS and had had tremendous success with that, which had greatly enhanced his reputation.

"Thank you, Doctor. I just don't see the point of dragging it out, if I'm going to be sick the entire time. Another two months, spent in my bed, wishing I was dead isn't much of a prize."

"You wouldn't be that ill, if we get the chemo dosage right. It's your choice of course, and I respect your decision. I'm not sure I would do anything differently myself in that situation. You're more than welcome to think about it, and get back to me if you change your mind. You might like to read a paper I wrote about A.L.L., and the work I've been doing. It might make a difference if you read more about it." He handed a copy of it to Alaistair, who folded it and put it in his pocket, and thanked the doctor. "You're not far away, in London. You could come over once every four weeks and get an interim dose mid-month in London. It won't debilitate you as much as you fear. And if it does, we can adjust the dose, or stop if you prefer." He gave Alaistair his personal cell number to call. The two men shook hands, and then Alaistair left, and walked back to his hotel from the Left Bank.

It was a beautiful day and he felt oddly buoyed by the meeting and more determined than ever to choose his own exit path, and the timing of it. The pills he kept nearby now gave him a sense of some control over his own destiny. He had no regrets about the choice he was making. It gave him a sense of freedom knowing that he wouldn't wither away as so many people he knew had. He felt oddly at peace as he walked through the Paris streets, and crossed the Alexandre III Bridge to the Right Bank. He walked past the Grand Palais, where he knew Gabrielle Gates was meeting with art dealers at the Biennale. He walked for a long time, and felt at ease when he got back to the hotel. He was surprised to see Gabrielle crossing the lobby toward him, as he headed back to his room to rest. The meeting with Professor Leblanc and the walk back to the hotel had drained him.

Gabrielle looked bright and alive in a red wool suit and high heels, with her dark hair pulled back. She smiled as soon as she saw him.

"You look lovely," he couldn't resist saying. There was something special about her. It was something warm and compassionate in her eyes, like a woman who had suffered acutely and had come out the other end without a trace of bitterness. He admired her for it.

"Thank you. I just had a text from Judythe," she answered. "Richard came through it. The surgery lasted until seven A.M., but they located the problem, and they think he's going to be all right. They're 'guardedly optimistic,' as she put it. They're going to keep him asleep all day, and she said she'd come back to the hotel to shower and change." Gabrielle looked relieved, and Alaistair smiled broadly. Richard was eleven years younger than he was, was about to get married, and wanted children. It seemed right that he get a new lease on life. But he didn't have a degenerative illness that would eat him alive from the inside. "Did you have your meeting yet?" she asked him.

"I did. I just finished," he said with a smile. "I walked past the Grand Palais on the way back, and thought of you. I assumed that you were there."

"I'm on my way now," she said, glancing at her watch. "Would you like a pass to join me there this afternoon?" He thought about it and the idea appealed to him, There was something very attractive about her.

"I'd like that," he said. "Can I interest you in dinner tonight in exchange?" She hesitated for only a fraction of a second and then nodded.

"That would be nice." Then she lowered her voice conspiratorially. "The maid told me this morning that someone was murdered in one of the suites on our floor last night. I heard a woman scream, I think you had already left to meet Judythe at the hospital. Apparently, it was one of the night maids who found the body. He wasn't the registered guest, but was the guest of a guest. They've kept it out of the paper so far, but that's a bit of excitement at the staid Louis XVI. They must be having fits over it. That can't be good for business," she said sympathetically.

81

"I wouldn't think so," he said, looking intrigued.

"The staff have been instructed not to talk about it, but the maid couldn't resist."

"Was it some kind of a mafia hit or a drug deal?"

"I have no idea, I don't think she knew. The police were all over the place for several hours."

"There were still some here when I got back last night. I didn't pay much attention to it. I thought it was just additional security."

"Well, they had a busy night last night, with Richard, and then a murder." She handed him a pass to the Biennale then, and told him which stand to meet her at and when, and then she hurried off. He was thinking about her as he headed back to his room. And as soon as he got there, he went to his bathroom, and opened the pouch where he was keeping the pills that he viewed as his ticket to freedom, when he would need them. They were his best friends now, and he knew he could count on them. He lay down on his bed then, and thought about what the professor had said that morning. He knew he could try the professor's particular protocol if he wanted to, but he didn't. He couldn't see the point of dragging things out, if he would be sick as a dog for his last months. He didn't believe the professor that he wouldn't be as ill as he feared, and would even be able to continue his medical practice if he wanted to, as long as he didn't overdo it. He thought his own solution was better, to sail out into the open seas slowly, unmedicated, and take the pills in the end. In any case, he still had time. A couple of months anyway. It was why he had come to Paris while he still felt well. He wanted to see it one last time.

* * *

Patrick checked the papers carefully that morning, but there was no mention whatsoever of the Russian male model who had died the night before at the Louis XVI. They were keeping it quiet for now, but Patrick was sure the investigation was still going full force, and would continue until they came to some conclusion about whether it was an accident, or if someone had murdered Sergei. For the moment they had no suspects, as far as Patrick knew, and no motive he was aware of. And in truth, it had been an accident. Sergei had tripped on his own. He had never intended to kill him, and hadn't laid hands on him, and even if he had been furious at Sergei for upping the ante on the blackmail money again, he would never have killed him. Sergei's fatal fall was an accident, even if he was a slime of the worst order.

It was a relief not to see it in the paper though, although Patrick knew some mention of it would be made eventually. Olivier Bateau knew it too, and was also praying that it had been an accident and not a homicide. He had felt sick since the night before.

Alaistair slept for two hours when he got back to his room, ordered a light lunch from room service, and put on a tie to meet Gabrielle at the Biennale. She had been so nicely dressed when he saw her in the lobby that he didn't want to embarrass her. She was very chic, and had an understated style he liked.

He met her at the booth she had mentioned and they walked around the Biennale art and antiques fair together, past booth after booth of museum quality antiques and important paintings. Booths set up by reputable dealers, and half a dozen major jewelers were represented too. It was an art fair of major proportions, and they enjoyed it. Most of the bigger dealers who dealt in high-priced art seemed to know Gabrielle, and she introduced Alaistair to all of them.

They went to the Bar Vendôme at the Ritz afterward for a drink, and from there he took her to one of his favorite restaurants for dinner. They had a lovely evening, and found plenty of things to talk about. The conversation never lagged for a moment. On their way to dinner, Judythe called Alaistair and reported that Richard was doing well, still asleep and heavily sedated, but they had already taken him off the respirator, and his new heart valve was performing well. She still sounded worried about him, but less so than she had the night before. She thanked him again profusely.

They walked home from the restaurant in the balmy September air. The city looked exquisite at night. They parted company finally, outside the door to Gabrielle's suite. They were both pleasantly tired, and Gabrielle had more meetings planned for the next day. She was staying for the week and Alaistair was too. He had assumed it was the last trip he'd be able to take and wanted to savor it. He said they'd have to do dinner again, which sounded good to her.

He had been surprised to feel energized for most of the day. He wasn't as tired as he had been lately. Paris had a magical effect on him, and Gabrielle said the same thing at dinner. She was feeling excited about her life and her work again, at forty-five, and said she had finally come out of the doldrums after her divorce. She was still young enough to have fun and a full life, and intended to do that from now on. She wanted to do some traveling, and she was pleased with the art purchases she had made for some of her clients that day. It had been a good day for both of them.

When Patrick got home that night, he didn't notice the two detectives waiting in an unmarked car outside his home. He let himself in to the apartment, and Alice was there. She had prepared dinner, and they were going to eat together, which was rare. The doorbell rang before they could sit down. It was Detectives Forrestier and Plante, who asked to speak to him again.

He took them into his study and told Alice he wouldn't be long. She didn't ask who they were, and assumed it was something related to his work. She was used to agents and detectives showing up to see him. He closed the door behind him, and sat down at his desk, as they took the two seats across from him, as they had the night before.

"I really have nothing to add," he told them, convinced that what he'd told them previously was airtight, and the case was nearly closed, except for whatever they found out about Sergei Karpov, and his unsavory connections.

"We came across a discrepancy in your story, and I want to make sure we understood you correctly," Detective Forrestier said quietly. "You mentioned that you didn't order any food while you were at the hotel. The room service records show that someone ordered caviar, foie gras, and vodka to the suite. You said you assumed if food was ordered, it would have been Karpov ordering it after you left, and that possibly he had used the suite to meet someone else once you were gone."

"I think that's probably what happened. Maybe they had an argument, and that person pushed him." Patrick volunteered the scenario he wanted them to believe.

"We checked again with the room service waiter on duty for your floor last night. He said he served the items I mentioned to an older man, with gray hair, who was wearing one of the hotel robes when he signed for it. He didn't recall the man's face. But the description sounds like you, Minister. We showed him one of Karpov's modeling photos, and a photograph of you again, and he wasn't certain but he tentatively identified you as the man who signed for the caviar and foie gras, wearing the bathrobe. What intrigues me about it is that he said you appeared to be alone in the suite, wearing a bathrobe. Did you shower before you met with Karpov? But if so, then why did you tell us that you hadn't ordered food? Or was Karpov actually there with you, in another room, the bedroom or bathroom of the suite? I'm puzzled by the lie about the food, and why you had your clothes off if he was there?" Detective Forrestier's eyes drove through Patrick's like power drills, and the minister of the interior was stunned into silence for a moment. "Would you care to explain that to me?"

"I must have forgotten about the food, I had other things on my mind," he said in a dull voice. His story was beginning to unravel. He had lied to the police about at least part of the story and they knew it. When he spoke to them the night before, he had forgotten about the food Sergei had ordered.

"Was there, in fact, another reason why you met with Karpov at the hotel?" If so, it made Patrick a possible suspect for the sperm spilled in the bed. They had taken the sheets as evidence, to test later, but hadn't done so yet. "Had you ever met Sergei Karpov at hotels on other occasions?" Patrick was stunned into silence again, and he realized that he had to come cleaner with them than he had the night before, to save his neck. The first story hadn't worked. And the truth might be his only option, or at least part of it. He felt like a cornered animal and was almost panting in terror, in contrast to his cool exterior. He could lie and claim that someone else signed for the food, another older man who was there after him, but he didn't want to get in any deeper than he was, with more lies.

He sounded breathless when he answered the detective, who hadn't taken his eyes off him for a second.

"It's something I have never wanted to admit to anyone. I got myself into a bad spot with Sergei Karpov. In confidence, I will admit to you that I committed . . . indiscretions with him on a few occasions." He almost cried when he said it. He had never exposed himself like this before, but now he had to. "It's not something I'm proud of, and no one has ever known. My wife doesn't know certainly. It would destroy her, and our marriage, if she knew. It's just something that has happened once in a great while, and I was foolish to commit a few of those indiscretions with Sergei Karpov. He knew who I was, and he began blackmailing me two years ago." Patrick didn't know that Forrestier had examined his bank records earlier that day, and he had questions about those too, if Patrick hadn't volunteered what he just did. He had suspected blackmail too. "I met with him at the hotel yesterday to pay him the next installment. In fact, he wanted to increase what I had agreed to pay him, and I told him I just couldn't."

"Did you have sex with him at the Louis XVI?" Forrestier asked him in an expressionless tone. Patrick hesitated for a long time before he answered. But he was cornered, and he knew they could prove it with DNA tests.

"Yes, I did," Patrick said in a broken voice.

"Did you pay him?"

"No, I didn't. I told him I couldn't." It was a variation of the truth. Since he had put the money back in his briefcase once Sergei was dead.

"Did you hit him, or he hit you? Did you argue?" Detective Forrestier pressed him.

"No."

"Was he alive when you left the room?"

"Yes." Patrick didn't dare tell them the whole story. They would think he had pushed him. He had told them enough.

Forrestier stood up then, and looked at Patrick. "Thank you for your honesty, Minister. I can't protect you or guarantee you confidentiality in a matter of this seriousness, when a man lost his life, no matter how unworthy he was or what a scumbag he was. The press will get their hands on some or all of this at some point. You need to prepare yourself for that, and be open with those close to you." He meant Patrick's wife, and Patrick got the drift. He nodded miserably, as he followed them to the door a few minutes later and let them out. Forrestier turned to him as he stood in the doorway. "We'll let you know how the investigation develops." Patrick just prayed it would stop there. But he had started a tidal wave, and he knew that it could drown him. Forrestier was right. He had to tell Alice now. He owed it to her. He couldn't let her read something like this in the newspaper. However disconnected they had become, he owed it to her to prepare her for the worst.

But the one thing he didn't realize, as he focused on the sexual aspects of the story, was that by telling the police that he and Sergei had been sexually involved, and Sergei had been blackmailing him, they had a motive for murder now. Sergei blackmailing him was the most damning evidence of all for Sergei's death being not an accident but a homicide.

There were tears bulging in Patrick's eyes as he walked into the kitchen, where Alice was waiting with dinner for him. He couldn't even swallow let alone eat, as he sank into a chair, and looked at her with tears of shame and regret rolling down his cheeks. He had everything on the line now, his job, his political career, the presidential election, his marriage, his family, and his freedom. He had risked it all with Sergei Karpov. He hated him with every ounce of his being as he looked at his wife, and braced himself to tell her the truth.

Chapter 6

P atrick knew he would never forget the look on his wife's face
when he told her that there had been times, rare, infrequent,
impossible to explain, when he had succumbed to some of man's
baser instincts and had gone to hotels, usually anonymously, to commit sexual acts with partners he scarcely knew. There had never been
anyone he had cared about though. He tried to put it as delicately as
he could. She stared at him in astonishment.

"You mean prostitutes?" she said, with an expression that was
puzzled as much as shocked. The real shock to her was that he was
confessing his guilt to her. She had suspected his infidelities for years,
presumably with other women.

"Yes, prostitutes, sometimes. Or just strangers. I never got involved with them. It was just something that happened on the spur
of the moment. It was never planned."

"Why are you telling me this now?" She had always guessed that
he wasn't faithful to her, but at least he was discreet. Whatever he

did, he kept away from her. But she had always sensed that there were others, right from the beginning. She tried not to think about it much, but felt that it had killed their marriage for her.

"I think I have to tell you," he said grimly, as she sat down at the kitchen table with him and stared at him with the same confused expression.

"Why now? I don't need to know who you cheated on me with. I always assumed there were other women. Most of the men we know aren't faithful to their wives. I've always preferred to look the other way." She knew her mother and grandmother had done the same. Most French men weren't faithful.

"There weren't other women," he said in a low growl. "You were wrong about that."

"But you just said . . ."

"They were men, Alice. Not women." Her mouth literally fell open when he said it. She looked like a fish, silently moving her mouth, with no sound coming out.

"They were *men*? You cheated on me with *men*?" It was the last thing she would have suspected him of. He was totally masculine, a man's man. She had never dreamed he would be attracted to his own sex. He always made his disgust for homosexuals clear. He was vocal about it, with no apology for his narrow point of view. "I never guessed that you were gay," she said, still trying to absorb it. She felt like she was going into shock, but she wasn't. She was entirely lucid and had heard him correctly. Alice lived in a black and white world, with very traditional views, which he had always claimed to share, both publicly and privately. He said during his campaigns that family values were essential to him and governed his life.

"I'm not gay," he shouted at her.

"Men who have sex with other men are gay. Even I know that," she said angrily. Why had he married her if he was gay? It explained why he hadn't touched or desired her in years.

"They were sexual acts, aberrations, that deviated from the norm, or the average person's behavior, but that doesn't make me gay. They were isolated acts. They didn't mean anything to me," he insisted, as though it made everything right. But he knew better, and he also knew that what he was telling her could ruin him if it got out, if she exposed him to get revenge for his rejection of her.

"Why *are* you telling me now?" she asked again, her eyes narrowing. Their marriage was already nearly dead or in a deep coma, so why did she need to know these sordid details? She couldn't guess what was to come next, but sensed that there might be more.

"I'm telling you because one of the men has been blackmailing me for the past two years."

"And you paid him? With what? *Our* money, *our* savings? An inheritance I don't know about?" His job was prestigious, but his salary wasn't enormous, and they had community property, as was the norm in France. She tried to save money and put it in a joint account. And he had spent it to buy the silence of a man he had slept with? The thought of it made her feel sick.

The rest came out in a rush. "I met him at a hotel yesterday to pay him off. Apparently, after I left, he fell and hit his head in the hotel room. They found him dead after I left. He either had an accident, or someone killed him. I didn't. I was gone by then. But the story will probably break in the press in the next day or two, and I didn't want you to read it in the newspaper. There's an inquiry going on, and an official police investigation. They kept it quiet today, but they won't be able to for much longer. I had to tell you.

"Once they deem the cause of death accidental, the whole thing will die down. But the shocker in the story will be that I've met men in hotel rooms, if that part of the story gets out. It depends how much is in the police report and what part of it is open to the public. The news channels and papers love stories like this. The police can't control what the media says, and neither can I. You need to brace yourself for the storm that could be coming. There's no way to guess what the press will say, and I have no control over them. No one does. So now you know about my sordid extramarital activities. I guess you should have known all along. I should have told you, but the time was never right. Not for this kind of news, Alice. And with what happened, I can't keep it from you any longer."

They both forgot about dinner as they sat silently on the kitchen chairs, each of them lost in their own thoughts. Alice was the first to break the silence, after she clattered the pots that were waiting and other objects around the kitchen, in her rage at him.

"After this blows over, I want a divorce," she said in a small, sure voice. "We should have divorced a long time ago. We need to do that now."

He looked deeply worried. "If there's anything left of my political career after this, you'll destroy it if you divorce me," he said, pleading with her.

"Are you joking? I feel sorry for you, Patrick. You've made a mess of our life, and your own. Remarkably, I don't hate you for it, but I won't stay married to you. This is too much." She was a deeply religious woman and he had violated her trust and all she believed in. He couldn't expect her to stay married to him.

He went back to his study then. He had warned her and told her all she needed to know. He was tired of lying, hiding, and dancing around the truth. It was what Sergei had preyed on, and others like him. Patrick didn't want to lead a life of secrets and deception anymore. This was what it led to.

Alice locked herself in their bedroom that night, and he slept in his study. He lay awake for most of the night, and finally fell asleep when the sun came up. She spent the night thinking about the fact that the soul of their marriage was finally dead now, if it ever had one. He had killed it. She felt free and sad all at the same time. She felt stupid for never suspecting that his sexual preference was men. It explained many of the things that had gone wrong between them, but he had concealed it well. And all the while, she thought, he had made a fool of her. She had stayed married to him for their children. And she wanted out now, for herself. She had lived in the way that suited him. Now it was her turn.

Patrick was sitting in the kitchen drinking a cup of coffee, in the clothes that he had slept in, when Detectives Forrestier and Plante rang their doorbell in the morning. The guardian had let them in downstairs. Alice was in the shower. He opened the front door, and saw the two men gazing straight at him. They took one step into the apartment and snapped handcuffs on him, and told him he was under arrest, as he stared at them, unable to believe what was happening.

"You're under arrest for the murder of Sergei Karpov," Inspector Plante said expressionlessly. Forrestier explained that they were putting him in *garde à vue,* a form of detention initially for twenty-four hours, which they could stretch to six days, while they continued to gather evidence against him to build their case. The prosecutor had not yet decided if they would ask for a charge of manslaughter, or first-degree murder, or something in between, or the investigating judge could ultimately decide it was an accidental death. They didn't have all the facts yet. But Patrick had a clear motive. He stood to gain from Sergei's death, to end his blackmail and the threat to Patrick's career and ambitions. They were lovers, and only death had stopped him. Patrick had everything to gain from Karpov's death. Whether or not the case held up would depend on the evidence that continued to turn up.

Alice came out in the hall in her bathrobe as they explained the charges to him. She heard voices and wondered what was going on. She arrived just in time to hear it, and tears filled her eyes as she looked at him, and realized how far he'd fallen. She was crying for herself and her children more than for him. She would have to tell them now. He always left the hard jobs to her. But at least he had warned her the night before. The humiliation for him was going to be total. But the police were convinced that this was more than just an accident and they were determined to prove it. They hadn't bought his story about a third party, or it happening after he left the hotel. Detective Forrestier felt in his gut that Patrick was lying about something.

Patrick kept saying over and over again, "I didn't push him," as they led him away, and Alice watched and then closed the door softly behind them. With her last glimpse of Patrick, she saw that there were tears on his cheeks. She felt sorry for him, but not enough to want to stay married to him, or forgive him.

The story was in the newspapers and on TV by the end of the day. Reporters on air announced that the minister of the interior had been arrested as part of a sex scandal that involved a Russian male model he had had a secret meeting with at the Louis XVI Hotel, and the male model was allegedly blackmailing him. They said that the Russian model had died in the course of their clandestine assignation, and the degree of the minister's involvement in his death was being investigated. The reporter said that their secret liaison had gone on for two years, which made it sound much more serious than a casual encounter.

Alice had managed to call her children first. Their daughter, Marina, was devastated and insisted that it had to be jealous lies in some sort of conspiracy against him, to keep him from the presidency. She could believe no ill of her father. He had been her hero all her life.

Their son, Damien, was livid at his father. He left his office to check on his mother, and found her shaken but holding up. Marina had offered to come home from Lille as well, but Alice didn't want her to, and told her to stay at the university. She didn't want the press following her children and hounding them. She wasn't leaving their apartment herself.

By the next morning, the situation was worse. Several more men had come forward and said they had had brief sexual encounters with Patrick, and had gone to hotels with him. One said he'd had sex with him in cheap hotels, and in a public men's room. The others wanted their moment of glory too. Most said they hadn't known who he was at the time, and he had given a false name, but they recognized him from the photographs now. Others had known his identity, or recognized him when they met.

The media requests for interviews or comments from Patrick had been turned down by the police. Patrick had contacted an attorney from jail.

Alice didn't go to visit him. He had tendered his resignation as minister of the interior through his lawyer. Even if the murder charges were ultimately dropped, the sex scandal aspect of it made it impossible for him to keep his position. For the moment anyway, his political career was over, probably forever. He would never recover from a scandal like this. Affairs with women were more easily accepted by the public, homosexual carnal exploits with young men were not, especially by a man whose public image was of a family man with wholesome values. He had been exposed as a hypocrite and a sexual deviate. Whether or not he was a murderer remained to be proven. In a matter of days, his whole life had been destroyed.

At the end of three days in jail under observation, a judge accepted the police's theories about him, set the charges as "involuntary homicide," i.e., manslaughter, and having fled the scene of the death he had caused. A trial date had not yet been set. The judge, after considerable negotiation, agreed to allow him to go free until the trial, with the proviso that he could not travel anywhere, and he would be checked on regularly by the police. All Patrick wanted was to hide in his apartment, shielded from view and public criticism.

Reporters were camped out in front of their apartment building. He had asked Alice to allow him a week or two to find a place to live.

She was adamant about his moving out as soon as he was released from jail. He looked like a broken man when she saw him again, and she kept to herself in the apartment, in order to avoid the press. She hadn't been out in days herself. Whatever they needed, like food, they had delivered.

On Patrick's first night home from jail, their son, Damien, came to see his father. The visit was traumatic for all of them. In the white heat of a barely controlled rage, Damien accused his father of being the scum of the earth, a hypocrite, a lowlife without morals, and a source of shame and humiliation for all of them. He had lied to the entire world.

"How dare you!" Damien roared at him. "With all your high and mighty hypocritical, pompous, homophobic bullshit. You have something vicious to say about every gay person you see on the street. I've known I was gay since I was sixteen, but I could never tell you because I was so afraid you'd hate me for it. And look at you, all the while you were meeting sleazy guys in hotel rooms and public bathrooms. It's all over the press. You're worse than anything you could say about me, Papa. And you're a murderer on top of it. How could you do this to our mother, to us, and disgrace us like this?" Patrick had no answers for him, he didn't even try. He apologized to his son, and was feeling deeply sorry for himself, more than for them. Damien's last words to his father before he left were "I hate you!" Alice was sobbing when her son walked out. She was heartbroken at the dissent Patrick had caused, her children's humiliation, and the anguish he was inflicting on them all. She had always sensed that her son was gay, but was too embarrassed to broach the subject with him, so she had ignored it. She felt she had let him down too.

Patrick looked devastated and he was in shock to learn that his son was gay. He felt it like a physical blow. It was a clean sweep. There was nothing left of Patrick's life by the end of the week. He cursed the day he had met Sergei, and blamed it all on him. In fact, Patrick had failed his family with his lies and double life.

Alice had no idea how the family would ever recover from the blow and the shame he'd caused them. Patrick's lawyer said it was more than likely that he would go to prison for involuntary manslaughter. He had betrayed his position, his country, his family, and a man was dead directly or indirectly because of him, whether he had laid hands on him or not. He warned Patrick that if they could find the evidence to prove premeditation, or that he had pushed Karpov before he fell, he would be charged with first degree murder, and he would go to prison for a long, long time, as long as thirty years. As it was, he was facing a sentence of up to ten years.

Patrick sat locked in his study, day after day, staring out the window, and thinking of all he had lost. He wished that he had the courage to commit suicide, but he didn't. It was all he could think about.

After a brief break, Alice was continuing to teach her classes, which her colleagues and students thought was brave of her and they admired her for it. She found a furnished apartment for Patrick nearby, and helped him move out. He wasn't capable of doing anything at the moment. She felt sorry for him and what his bad decisions, self-indulgence, and compulsions had cost him, but she no longer wanted him in their home. She couldn't forgive the lies that she realized had gone on for years. And for Patrick, the black cloud around him obscured everything. All he could think about was what he had lost, more than how badly he had hurt them. Alice saw now how ego-driven and narcissistic he was. She told him she would wait to file the divorce until after the trial, but there was no question in her mind. She was going to end the marriage and was sorry she hadn't done it years before.

There was peace for her in the decision she had made. She had nothing left to give him, after having forgiven so much for so long, and tolerating how little he had given her for years. She had made excuses for him to their children, and to herself. One of his campaign slogans was "The Family Man." He had turned their life and their marriage into a cruel joke. He was paying the price for all of it now, or he would. Alice was convinced that Patrick deserved whatever happened to him. Only Patrick believed he was the victim.

Alaistair and Gabrielle visited Richard at the hospital on the second day after his surgery, and he was doing well. Judythe was with him, and hadn't left him for a minute, except to grab fresh clothes at the hotel. She was struggling with her French, talking to the nurses, and making herself understood, and Richard looked healthier than they'd expected. He had "pinked up" nicely. It struck Gabrielle that three days before, none of them had known one another and now they felt like friends. Alaistair and Gabrielle had shared several meals, he was fascinated by her involvement in the art world, and she enjoyed his company. Sharing Richard's near-death experience had reminded both of them of how precious life was, and how fleeting, and they were seizing the moment together.

They all talked about the sex scandal that had occurred right in the hotel while Richard was fighting for his life and they were trying to save him. They were shocked by the accidental death of the Russian male model who was allegedly blackmailing the minister of the interior and presidential hopeful.

"He must be one very unhappy guy," Alaistair commented. "It sounds like one of those moments when all the stars collide and it brings the house down. Supposedly, he was a very respected politician and probably would have won the election next year. Now, people think he'll go to prison. I guess he's just another dishonest politician, but it's really a tragedy. A young man is dead, the minister's wife and kids must be horrified, and a dignified career is in rubble at his feet. You wonder what he was thinking."

"Pure self-indulgence probably," Richard answered, "and he never thought he'd get caught."

"Typical politician," Judythe said with a shrug. She knew that the nurses were all talking about it, and it was in the newspapers. She didn't feel sorry for him. It sounded like a disgusting story to her, and she felt sorry for his wife and kids. There were photographs of them in the papers too, and they looked like decent people. There was a picture that had been taken only that summer with Patrick and Alice smiling and their children on either side of them at a Fourteenth of July celebration in the South of France. And all the while Patrick was paying blackmail to a sleazy male lover, to protect himself. Gabrielle hated men like him. The public agreed with her and their sympathies were entirely with his wife and family.

Richard was going to spend the rest of the week in the hospital recuperating, and then two more weeks back at the hotel, before they would release him to go back to New York. He had to see a heart surgeon there, he explained to Alaistair and Gabrielle. The cardiac surgeon in Paris had told him that he could go back to work four weeks after the surgery. His frightening episode had extended their stay in Paris by more than two weeks, and they'd had to cancel their trip to Rome. The Louis XVI had given them a special rate for the extra two weeks, since they were obliged to stay for medical reasons.

"We'll save Rome for our honeymoon," he said, smiling at Judythe. "We haven't figured out the date yet, but we want you both to come to our wedding. There wouldn't be one if it weren't for you," he said to Alaistair. "And my future wife. The two of you saved my life." His heart anomaly had turned out to be one of those which surface brutally, with no warning signs, and usually killed some previously healthy-seeming young person on the spot, often while exercising, and left their loved ones in shock.

"It was a team effort," Alaistair reminded him modestly, "Judythe and I and the very wonderful medical personnel of the SAMU, and then your surgeon and his team here. They tell me you shouldn't have any trouble after this. It's a one-time occurrence when the repair is successful, and your new valve shouldn't give you any trouble. It'll be smooth sailing from here."

"I'm counting on it," he said, as he kissed Judythe, sitting on the bed next to him. It pleased them both to see Gabrielle and Alaistair together. They seemed so well suited and compatible that it looked like the perfect match. Judythe and Richard wondered if it would continue after they left respectively for London and New York. It was obvious that they were happy now. Where it went after that, it was too soon to tell. And they lived an ocean apart, which was complicated.

Gabrielle and Alaistair had dinner at a restaurant new to both of them that night. They served a combination of French and Thai food, and it was delicious. After the meal, Gabrielle caught Alaistair looking wistful, and staring into space for a moment. He seemed sad, and then he recovered himself and smiled at her. She looked at him quizzically.

"You looked so sad for a minute," she said softly. "Are you okay?" He did that sometimes, and seemed to drift off, his mind a million miles away.

"I was just thinking how sorry I am that I didn't meet you earlier." She was the kind of woman he would have wanted to have fallen in love with on the first round. It seemed so cruel to meet her now that it was too late. He had so little time left, according to the doctors, and he knew it wouldn't be fair to pull her into a romance with him, only to abandon her a few months later. In good conscience, he couldn't do that to her, but they were enjoying each other and spending so much time together.

She had taken him with her to an appointment with an art dealer that afternoon about a painting at the Biennale, and he was impressed when he saw her negotiate. She had refined the process to a fine art, and got the result she wanted. She had played the dealer like a violin. She got the painting her client in New York wanted, and a better deal on it than he dared to hope for.

"I always get my man," she said with a wicked grin, after they left the fair. The painting was being shipped to New York. "You have wonderful art fairs in London," she commented. "I used to go to every single one. I've done a lot less traveling in the last two years, but I'm back in the groove again."

"I hope so," Alaistair said softly. "I'd love to meet up with you in London." Or meet her in New York, or any of the places she traveled to. She was a moving target.

She hadn't mentioned Alaistair to her daughters. It seemed much too soon to tell anyone anything. Who knew where it would all go in the coming months? She could sense that they wanted their budding relationship to continue, but they were both being very cautious about what they said to each other, and didn't want to be presumptuous. And long-distance relationships were difficult at best.

The subject came up at dinner at an Indian restaurant the next day. Going to fancy restaurants every night was expensive, and exhausting, and they enjoyed the little bistros more. Alaistair insisted on paying for the dinners, and Gabrielle was touched. They had both held back about saying too much about the future. They lived worlds apart, across an ocean, and had demanding careers. Gabrielle's work was more flexible. Her clients were all over the world. But Alaistair had patients counting on him daily in London.

"Why is it that I get the impression that there is something you're not telling me?" she asked him cautiously, and he took a long time to answer. And suddenly she realized the most likely reason for it. He was European after all. "Are you married?" she asked him, looking worried, and he smiled.

"No. I'm divorced. I have been for fifteen years." But she could sense that there was something he wasn't saying. Maybe he had a serious girlfriend. It wouldn't be surprising. He was a good man.

"Sorry . . . I just had a feeling. I didn't mean to pry."

"You're welcome to pry, or even ask me," although he wasn't sure what he'd answer. He didn't want to lose her before they had a chance to get to know each other better. "I've been sick for the past four months," he finally admitted.

"Seriously sick?"

"I guess you could call it that. At least my doctors say so, although doctors can be wrong. I came to Paris to meet with a very famous research professor, to discuss a rare form of blood disease they say I have. The tests have been pretty conclusive, I was probably wasting my time. I went to see the professor on Monday."

"And?" Gabrielle's perfectly smooth skin furrowed on her forehead. He thought she was exquisite. Beautiful *and* smart. He couldn't have done better if he'd looked a lifetime for her. Instead, he had found her across the hall in a Paris hotel.

"The professor agrees with my doctors in London, about the diagnosis. He uses a different protocol to treat the disease. He's developing it, supposedly with good results. The treatment is very aggressive. I've seen too many of my friends and patients suffer the agonies of the damned and destroy the quality of life they have left. I've decided not to do that. I'm going to enjoy the coming months for as long as they last, and then I'm going to ride quietly into the sunset. No fuss, no bother, no hideous treatments and ghastly end of life. I'm not willing to sign on for that."

"Can it be cured?" There were tears in her eyes when she asked him. She felt terrible for him.

"Sometimes. Rarely, but it happens. If you're lucky, you can drive the disease into remission. But the statistics on it are discouraging. I turned the professor down, and I'm not sorry I did. Except now, when I look at you. But I want to enjoy you for as long as I can. I don't want to be sick, and in my bed sicker from the treatment than from the disease."

"But if you can get it into remission, isn't it worth it?" she reasoned with him.

"I don't think so. And the chances of that happening are minimal." He was realistic about it.

"Never mind the statistics. If you're the lucky one here, and get it into remission, you'll have a life, Alaistair, without the sword of Damocles hanging over your head."

"It would always be there. And that isn't what I want to do," he said gently, and changed the subject. But the topic he had brought up haunted them for the rest of the meal, and his words hung between them. "I watched both my parents die slow, horrible deaths while they fought to stay alive. I don't think the awful treatments they endured gave them more than a few days or weeks, under terrible conditions. I'm not going to do that, Gabrielle."

"So, what are you going to do? Just ignore it?" There was an edge to her voice when she asked him, and he smiled when he answered.

"I'm going to enjoy my life, and spend every moment I can with you, until we leave here. Then I'm going back to London to see my patients, and you'll go back to New York and buy spectacular paintings for your clients, and we'll remember these days forever. I know I will." She could see that he meant it.

"And that's all? We won't see each other again? This is just a memory you're building? Don't you want more than that, Alaistair? Why won't you fight for your life? You're bigger than this disease."

"I doubt that I am. There are some battles you can't win. Sometimes you have to know that." She looked angry when he said it.

"If that was true, I would have just curled up and died when Arthur left me for that little idiot. He took all the joy and fun and love and my future with him, along with all our happy memories. I thought my life was over for about a year, and then I realized that he doesn't own my happiness. It doesn't belong to him. He can share whatever he wants now with his child bride, but I still have a right to be happy and fulfilled, even without him. I have a right to a good life too. He doesn't own anything to do with me, and he can't take it away and deprive me of it. That's why I came back to stay at the hotel we used to love, because he doesn't own that either, and he can't take it away from me, or cheat me of it. And look what happened when I came here. I met you. It's taken me almost three years to feel good about life again, but now I do. And I would fight to the death anyone who tries to take that away from me again. Look at Richard and Judythe. They had to fight their way out of two marriages to get where they are now. Alaistair, it's worth it." He looked pensive and then shook his head.

"Health matters are different," he said.

"It's all the same, health, love, or a person who is trying to rob you of something. Don't rob yourself. If there's even a chance that the professor here could get the disease into remission, why don't you try it? What have you got to lose? If it makes you feel too awful, you can stop taking it." That was what the professor had said to him too. And all he could think about now was where the pills were that he had brought with him, and had carried everywhere, so he could make a fast exit from life whenever he wanted to. He had consented to death, and given up on life, but now he was tempted to listen to her. In some ways, she made sense.

"I'll think about it," was all he'd concede, and changed the subject again. They walked past Notre-Dame all lit up on their way home from dinner, as the Eiffel Tower sparkled magically on the hour. And when they stood outside her room when they got back to the hotel, he tried to kiss her and she wouldn't let him.

"I'm not going to let you make me fall in love with you, Alaistair, and break my heart because you won't fight for whatever chance at life you have. I won't let you do that to me. I'm willing to take a chance with you and see what happens, but not if you just throw it all away." It was a lot to ask, but he was touched by what she'd said. He nodded and took a step back, and she slipped quietly into her room, and locked the door behind her. She had a right to make that decision.

When he got back to his own room, he walked into his bathroom, and looked at the pill bottles he had lined up on the shelf. They were his exit plan, his escape route to end a terrible fate. Until now, they had been his friends. They would help him avoid an agonizing end of life. She was asking him to turn his back on them, and cast his lot with life again. It was so much to ask, and it was already so late in the day. He didn't know if he had the strength to do what she was asking for. The little bottles of pills would be so much easier. And he knew he could count on them when the disease took over and he wanted out. He could feel Gabrielle pulling him toward her, but he was afraid to reach out. And she'd been wrong about one thing when she said he had nothing to lose. He had everything to lose, now that he'd met her.

Chapter 7

Gabrielle and Alaistair shared a last dinner together on Friday. She had to have dinner with a group of art dealers the next day, on her last night in Paris. They had spent some wonderful evenings together, and had many interesting conversations, in the city they both loved. There was a bittersweet feeling to their last dinner. She knew now that he was sick and didn't intend to fight it. He had a right to make that decision, but she had a right to not enter into it with him. She didn't want to stand by and watch him let himself die, or commit suicide as his "exit plan." It was just rotten luck to have met someone she liked so much, and was so attracted to, whose fate was sealed by a fatal illness he probably couldn't beat, and refused to fight. He thought it was more dignified to accept his fate and not engage in a battle he couldn't win. Neither of them mentioned it again at their last dinner.

They lingered for a long time at the bar at the hotel when they walked back, and they both noticed a famous rock star in the lobby surrounded by his entourage. He had given a concert the night before, and was on a world tour. He looked like a wild man, with long blond hair to his waist, tattoos up and down his bare arms and a tattoo of a gun on his face, and his long lean body was encased in black leather. He was bare-chested and wearing a leather vest. He was about Gabrielle's age, and she commented as they walked into the bar that Monsieur Lavalle, the manager who had retired, would never have allowed Declan Dragon into the hotel, let alone to stay there.

Alaistair smiled at her comment. Dragon was Irish, and one of the biggest punk rock stars in the world. "It would be hard not to let him stay here. The waiter who brought my breakfast this morning said that they have twelve rooms on the top floor, and the biggest suite in the hotel. That's big money to turn down."

"He looks like he just got out of prison," she said primly. He laughed and they walked into the bar, sat down at a cozy corner table, and spent two hours talking. She hated to say goodbye to him. Their meeting in Paris had been serendipitous, and she had enjoyed every minute of it. It had reminded her that there were still wonderful people in the world, and attractive men, even if she never saw him again. She hated the thought that he might not have long to live, and wasn't willing to do anything about it. It didn't seem noble to her, but a terrible waste, but she said nothing about it to him that night.

They were both walking slowly when they got to her room, dragging out the time, and she was tempted to abandon herself to him, and seize the moment. But reason won out. They stopped in front of her door, and before she could open it with her key, he kissed her.

She felt a thrill race through her and kissed him back, but let it go no further.

"Take care of yourself, Gabrielle, and thank you for spending time with me here. I know you were busy." But whenever they were together, it seemed as though they had all the time in the world.

"I should be saying that to you, and it worked out perfectly. I got everything done that I needed to." It had worked well for both of them. It occurred to her then that he was the first man she had kissed since Arthur. She suddenly felt a wave of sadness wash over her, at the thought of leaving him, and maybe never seeing him again. "I'll call you when I come to London for an art fair." She wanted to believe he'd still be alive and be there.

"I'll call you long before that," he promised. And a moment later, she slipped into her room, and he went to his own, thinking about her, and everything she'd said to him.

She left early the next morning for meetings, and was busy all day. She called Judythe and wished them luck, and they said they'd call her and get together in New York.

The trip had been so much better than Gabrielle had hoped, and she was glad that she had decided to do it. It had been the most fun she'd had in a long time. She felt free and independent after traveling alone, and making new friends.

Dinner with the art dealers went late that night, and she finished packing when she went back to the hotel. Alaistair called her on her cellphone in the cab on her way to the airport the next morning, and wished her a safe flight. He said he had decided to stay another day, and had some things left to do the next day. They hung up when she got to the airport.

He walked along the Seine for a long time that afternoon, and when he got back to his hotel room, he made the call to the number he'd been given. There had been an army of ragtag-looking people in the hotel lobby when he walked in. They were surrounded by mountains of band equipment. There were twenty or thirty people and Declan Dragon at the center of it. They had a bus waiting outside. There were hotel management personnel standing in a long line of frowning faces, and the next morning in the paper, Alaistair discovered why. Declan and his entire group had trashed their rooms to the point that the rooms would have to be put out of service for several months and redone. They had torn fabrics from the wall, broken picture frames and lamps in drunken brawls. The curtains had been torn down, and it had become a game in their inebriated drugged-out state. They had flung food at the walls and burned the carpet. The hotel management had asked them to leave, but they were leaving for London anyway.

When Alaistair went to his appointment the next morning, Olivier Bateau and Yvonne Philippe were in a meeting with their construction crew. They wanted an estimate of all the work that had to be done, and were going to send it to Declan Dragon's production manager. They were figuring it at just over a hundred thousand dollars. They had even set fire to an antique rug they'd rolled up and put in a bathtub. It had been wanton destruction, and Olivier Bateau was nearly in tears when he turned to his assistant after the meeting.

"We've been open for less than two weeks, and we've had a heart attack, an accidental death which was possibly murder, and nearly a whole floor destroyed by a rock star. I don't know if I'm up to this," he said.

"You'll get used to it," Yvonne reassured him. "We had worse at some of the hotels I worked for. Rock stars are a bad business. They always destroy their rooms. We even had a herd of goats delivered to a Middle Eastern royal family, who wanted the chef to slaughter them and serve them for dinner."

"I hope it calms down after this, before I have a heart attack, or the owners kill me," Olivier said nervously.

"They know what this business is like, even in a five-star hotel." Olivier Bateau also knew now why the famous Louis Lavalle had run the place with an iron hand. He would never have allowed the Irish rock star to stay there.

"I was trying to be modern and cool." The story of Dragon's destruction was all over the press, and the owners weren't going to like that either.

Olivier had a brief conversation with the owners that afternoon. They were most upset by the press coverage, and there was still a wall of paparazzi hanging around outside, waiting to see what celebrity would show up next. The owners of the Louis XVI had told Olivier in no uncertain terms that the next time a rock star, no matter how famous, tried to book rooms in the hotel, they were to be told that there were no rooms available, and he had promised to do that. They were very distressed about Sergei Karpov's death there earlier in the week as well, although they knew the minister of the interior personally, and were shocked by the stories about him, and the fact that he was being tried for homicide. It had been a very stressful week.

Alaistair was back in his room by then. The professor had been surprised to get his call early that morning, but had agreed to see him. The treatment had gone smoothly, and they established a schedule for his future treatments. He was going to come to see the professor every four weeks for treatment and evaluation, with an additional dose of the medication given every two weeks, administered by his oncologist in London.

"We'll see how you do on that schedule," the professor said kindly. His bedside manner had proven to be warmer than expected. "May I ask what made you change your mind?" he asked, curious. He always liked to know his patients' motivation, and thought that their state of mind had a marked effect on the treatment, and how well it was tolerated.

"I met a woman," Alaistair answered honestly, and the professor smiled.

"That sounds like an excellent reason to me. She's had a good influence on you. I think you made the right decision. Did you tell her?" Alaistair shook his head.

"No, I didn't. I wanted to see how things go first."

"That's a wise decision too."

He was going back to London and his own practice the next day. He thought about Gabrielle as he sat on the Eurostar and watched the countryside slide by at high speed. He wondered when and if he'd see Gabrielle again. All he could do was wait and see now, about her, and if the treatment worked. If not, and he got worse, he wasn't going to call her. So far there had been no ill effects, but it was too soon to tell. But he felt energized and more hopeful after the trip to Paris, and after they arrived in St. Pancras station, he went straight to his office. He had more compassion for his patients now that he was sick himself.

Complications

Gabrielle had called her daughters, Georgina and Veronica, once each during her week in Paris. Georgie was a senior at Georgetown in Washington, D.C., and loving it. Veronica had graduated from USC the year before, and had stayed in L.A. to work at the Getty Museum. She shared her mother's passion for art. Both girls were close to each other, though very different, and they were close to their mother, but hungry for their independence. They were very attached to their father too, and despite their initial anger over the divorce, and their dislike for Sasha, his new wife, whom they found unbearable, they had forgiven him. They simply ignored their twenty-six-year-old step-mother when they were with her, and their infant half brother. Their loyalty was to their mother, but their father had always been their hero. Handsome, sophisticated, successful, brilliant, they had wor-shipped him, with their mother's encouragement, since they were very little, and Gabrielle knew they loved her too. She had never been jealous of their relationship with their father. She had encour-aged it. During the first year of strife after the divorce, they had kept their distance from both parents and embraced their newfound in-dependence. They wanted their own lives now, separate and distant from their parents' problems.

Their living away from home now had given Gabrielle new inde-pendence too. It was not always welcome, and she was lonely at times in the apartment alone, but it was forcing her to develop her own life, without Arthur and the girls for the first time. She had dis-tanced herself from their old friends during the divorce, and she was hungry to meet new people and repopulate her life.

She called Veronica and Georgie the night she got back to New

York, and told them about the trip, without mentioning Alaistair. He was the first man who had appealed to her in years, but they didn't need to know that, and she had no desire to share that with them, and open herself up to criticism. And how could she explain that she had fallen for a man who had a potentially fatal disease, and possibly only months to live? It was much too complicated for a twenty-one- and twenty-three-year-old. It was even complicated for her. No matter how well suited they seemed for each other, he was still a stranger to them, and Gabrielle knew that they would see him as their father's rival. She hadn't challenged them with a dating life of her own since the divorce, and didn't intend to now. She and Alaistair didn't live in the same city and they had no plans to see each other. He was just something very lovely that had happened to her during a week in Paris. That was enough for now, and maybe forever. Gabrielle wasn't thinking about the future, and in the circumstances, he would have been the wrong man to do that with. He didn't appear to have a future.

She got busy with her work immediately, and she met with the clients she had purchased art for at the Biennale. In several cases, she had bought pieces that weren't on display there, but had been shown to her by galleries she did business with regularly.

The girls had no plans to come home before Thanksgiving. Georgie had just gone back to Washington, D.C., before Gabrielle left for Paris.

For Christmas, they were planning to go to the Turks and Caicos with their father, or possibly Saint Barts if he chartered a boat there. The girls had grown up in golden circumstances, but both had a serious social conscience, encouraged by their parents. It was Sasha,

Arthur's new wife, who was the spoiled brat in their midst, which they chose to overlook. They considered her their father's folly. She was beautiful, and cunning, and knew how to look out for herself, which she had learned on the streets of Moscow, but her lack of upbringing and manners showed in every situation. They couldn't understand why their father wasn't embarrassed by her. He found her charming, and treated her like an additional daughter, since she was almost the same age they were, and only slightly older than Veronica. Sasha was their contemporary, not their father's. He was forty-four years older than his wife. The baby she'd had with Arthur was a transparent ploy for financial security. She had two nannies for the infant, so she never had to spend a minute with him. Arthur was excited about having a son, although he spent little time with him too. But the baby was well cared for. They had named him Graham.

Gabrielle thought of them at times, although she tried not to. She remembered how different it was when she and Arthur had had their babies. Gabrielle was devoted to them, and they had been the hub of her life, the center of her universe. His marriage to Sasha was very different, the indulgence of an old man. She wondered at times how long it would last, but reminded herself that it was none of her business. He had a much fuller life than she did now, with a young wife, a baby, two older daughters, and his venture capital firm. Gabrielle had her work, her daughters when she saw them, and a solitary life now, since the divorce. She had gotten used to it, but it had taken time. She was more alone than lonely, and recognized the difference. Being on her own didn't frighten her now as it had in the beginning.

She had refused to let it destroy her when Arthur left her. The trip to Paris was the first major evidence of that, and she was glad she had gone. Meeting Alaistair had been the icing on the cake, not the main event, and she had concluded some very impressive deals while she was there. Arthur had never been particularly interested in her business, but he hadn't objected to it either, and now she was glad she had it. She would have been lost without it, with nothing to fill her days and occupy her.

Once back in New York, she rapidly settled into the routine of talking to her most important clients regularly, calling her daughters every few days and catching up on their news, following major auctions, and doing a great deal of reading to keep abreast of developments and events in the art world.

She thought of Alaistair frequently at night after the trip, but didn't call him. He had said he'd call her, and she assumed he would. If he came to New York, or she contacted him when she went to London, she'd be happy to see him, but she couldn't count on it, given his health and the death sentence he'd been given. She tried not to think of it, or even of him too often. She didn't want to get too attached to someone who might not even be alive in a month or two. She couldn't allow herself to become dependent on him.

Once Patrick Martin had been released from his few days in jail, and was back home, Detectives Forrestier and Plante had continued to call on him. They had dropped by without advance notice. Additional evidence in the case had surfaced, though nothing that altered the trajectory of the case. It had been confirmed, with DNA tests of the sheets, that he and Sergei had had sex at the hotel, which he had admitted to them anyway. Several times, they'd tried pressuring him into admitting that he had laid hands on Sergei and pushed him, but he remained staunch in his denial of that. The detectives couldn't prove otherwise, and for now they believed him.

Patrick had appeared more depressed each time they saw him. Everything that mattered to him had been stripped away, as a result of his disastrous involvement with the Russian male model, and his untimely death.

And eventually Patrick had had to face his daughter. Marina had come home from Lille for a weekend, and sobbed in her father's arms when she got there. She was devastated for him over the public humiliation he had suffered, the loss of his job and dignity and the respect of the entire country. Even if he was exonerated, by some miracle, or found innocent, it was clear that he would no longer have even the remotest possibility of becoming president. His reputation had been tarnished irreparably for life.

"Oh, Papa . . . I'm so sorry," she'd said, crying with his arms around her. She was the only member of the family who didn't blame him for his unsavory associations and acts, which were public knowledge now. Instead, she saw him as the victim, as Patrick did himself. She was, above all, his ally, which infuriated her brother, who accused her of being brainwashed, and blind to their father's faults and crimes. The possibility of his going to prison broke her heart.

With both of their children at opposite extremes, Alice rose to the occasion and was the voice of reason in their midst. She remained clear about how shocking their father's behavior had been, but she was compassionate. She was a living example of Christian compassion. She wanted nothing more to do with him herself, but she respected the fact that he was still her children's father, and he knew that Marina at least loved him. Damien was brimming with fury and resentment, and Patrick was still crushed that his son was gay, despite his own actions, which he considered aberrations and sexual acts, but not indications of his own homosexuality, which he continued to deny to them, and mostly to himself.

It was the darkest time of Alice's life, as she watched their family come apart like a machine breaking down and disintegrating in front of her eyes, and she did her best to keep her children together. Her work at the university was her salvation. Patrick was in his own small apartment by then, living on his limited savings. And he was spending the rest on lawyers. If convicted, he would no longer have his license to practice law either, after he got out of jail. He had no idea what he would do for a job. He could no longer envision the future. Seeing his lawyer, speaking to the police, and dealing with the upcoming trial were all consuming and were his only occupations.

It was hard for Alice to maintain a semblance of normalcy in the midst of it, but at least she no longer had to see him in the apartment. She was just grateful that her parents weren't alive to see what had happened. They were deeply proper and moral, and it would have killed them. She constantly asked herself how she could have married a man like him, but he had deceived her right from the beginning.

Patrick's mother was still alive, but had suffered from dementia for many years, and was in a home for the elderly in the South of France in Mougins. Patrick had visited her there occasionally, but he didn't now.

The police discovered evidence that Sergei had blackmailed at least two other men he had had relations with, which Patrick found encouraging, as damning evidence of his character. But when he asked his attorney about it, Gérard Pelaprat said it made no difference and would do nothing to help Patrick's case.

"It doesn't matter who else he blackmailed. *You* still had the motive to kill him. He was blackmailing *you*. You were angry about it, and you were in the room with him when he died." The police had the whole story now, and it didn't look good for Patrick. Patrick Martin was no longer either a respectable nor a sympathetic figure. He had lied to his wife for years, had a seamy life, with dubious sexual practices carried out in secret, and he had hidden his homosexuality from his family and the public, and had consorted with distasteful, dishonest, criminal people. Very little good could be said about him. He had been a fraud for his entire political career, damning homosexuals while secretly being one.

Alice had seen an attorney herself by then, to set up the divorce, but she had asked him to wait to file it with the court until after the trial. She said she didn't want to make things any worse than they already were for her husband. Marina was furious with her mother for divorcing him, and condemned her for it. She had all the naïveté of youth, along with her hero worship of her father.

"My God, we must be the most dysfunctional family on the planet," Damien said one night when he came to have dinner with his mother, after Marina was back at college in Lille. He worried about his mother, but she was holding up better than he had expected. She was braver than he'd thought.

"I'm sure there must be other families just as bad, or worse," she said, smiling at him. They were closer than they'd ever been, since the holocaust surrounding Patrick. It was a relief for both Damien

123

and his mother to acknowledge the fact that he was gay. There were no secrets between them anymore.

"Not really," Damien commented. "My father's been secretly gay all his life, sneaking around in cheap hotels, he's going on trial for the murder of one of his lovers. He lied to you, and my sister still thinks he walks on water. Could it get any worse?" he said ruefully.

"Probably," Alice said. "I just hope it doesn't. You have to play the hand you're dealt, Damien. We'll get through this. The world won't forget it, but they'll be distracted by other things eventually. This won't be the hot topic forever. And sadly, one day Marina will have to accept that her father made some terrible mistakes, and wasn't fair or honest with any of us."

"You in particular. I'm sorry, Maman, that you have to go through this," Damien said with feeling.

"It won't kill me. I'm worried about him. He has nothing left that he cares about or to live for. That's dangerous." Damien nodded and didn't comment. He had thought of it himself, and worried that his father might be a suicide risk. As angry as he was at his father, he didn't want anything worse to happen to him. Although he was putting them all through hell now. But Damien was proud of his mother for her strength and dignity. She never complained or bemoaned her fate or maligned their father to them, although Damien could see how deeply hurt she was. He knew it couldn't have been easy for her to realize that their entire marriage had been fraudulent, and Patrick had lied to her since the day he married her. Other than her children, she had wasted half a lifetime with him, as she saw it. She had started going to church every day, and it brought her some comfort. But you could feel the tension in the house mount as they wended their way slowly toward the trial. It had been set for January. It was going to be the longest four months of their lives. And somehow, she had no idea from where, Alice managed to dredge up the strength she and her children needed from the deepest part of her. She was living testimony to the strength and endurance of the human spirit.

Chapter 8

Gabrielle remained silent since she and Alaistair had left each other in Paris. She needed time to digest what had happened, and what he had told her. She didn't want to make commitments she couldn't live up to, or get into a situation she couldn't handle. According to what he said, and how he intended to deal with it, he was a dying man. She couldn't afford to be foolish, and sacrifice herself, or her sanity, for a man she barely knew. Even if from a distance, her daughters needed her. Arthur had shaken her to her core when he left her suddenly, and it had taken almost three years for her to recover from it. She couldn't risk herself again now for a man she had known for a week, no matter how lovely he seemed. She liked everything about him, except his rigid refusal to fight the battle at hand, and his determination to go down with the ship, perhaps sooner than necessary, by refusing treatment.

Alaistair called Gabrielle two weeks after she left Paris. She could hear how tired he was. He sounded exhausted when he called, but in good spirits. She wondered if his condition had worsened, but didn't want to bring up painful subjects and ask. He said that his medical office had been busier than usual with an outbreak of flu, which had hit early this year.

"Is that dangerous for you, to be exposed to your patients?" she asked him, trying not to sound like she was unduly worried, or mothering him. She didn't know him well enough to do that.

"I've been wearing a mask," he said, smiling at her concern. "I've brought in an assistant to see the worst cases. I'm spending most of my time with the healthy patients, for vaccines and routine check-ups. I feel like a bit of a wimp, but it's just smarter, especially now."

"Because of your illness?" she asked gently.

"Because I'm in treatment," he said quietly. "I'm not a total idiot. Everything you said made sense. You were right. I need to at least put up a fight. How can I expect my patients to, if I don't set an example for them? For years I've referred them for treatments I was too cowardly to face myself when confronted by the same challenge. I went back to see the professor the day after you left Paris."

She was stunned, and had tears in her eyes. "You did that? Oh, Alaistair, you're a brave man."

"No, I'm not, but you gave me courage. I was being a coward." And now he had something to live for. On his solitary walks along the Seine, he had realized that he had been coasting for years. His divorce had disheartened him years before. It had never been a great love or the right marriage, and they both knew it. But his having misjudged it so badly had taken something from him, his sense of hope, and faith in the future, and in an astonishingly short time, Gabrielle had helped him to find it again, within himself. "It may not work, but I decided to give it a try. He has the best success rate in Europe with the particular form of leukemia I have, and he's done the most thorough research. There are one or two very good men in the States too, but Paris is closer to home. I'll be seeing him once a month for six months, with a slightly milder cocktail administered in London mid-month. It's a nasty business, but if it works, it will have been worth it. You gave me the courage to do it, Gabrielle. Somehow not having children, and no one dependent on me, I thought it didn't matter. But I was wrong. It always matters. Life is precious, and every day is a gift. Thank you for reminding me of it. I was actually calling to ask you something. I don't know how you'll feel about it." No matter how pleasant their time together had been in Paris, they hardly knew each other. "I have to go back to Paris in two weeks for the next treatment. Would you meet me there? I know you're busy, but I thought I'd ask. If it makes you uncomfortable, I understand. I just hate to waste the time in Paris, without someone to share it with. That someone being you."

His unexpected invitation broadsided her completely. She hadn't expected it, and didn't know how to respond. It was one thing to urge him to be responsible, not give up hope, and give the treatment a try, it was another thing, and a much bigger one, to stand by him while he did it, even if she didn't go to the doctor with him, and take on a role she didn't feel ready for. She hardly knew him. It was more than just a few days in Paris. It was a deep commitment, to be his ally and support system. She didn't know what to answer and didn't want to hurt his feelings or discourage him. But if she met him there, it seemed like a big statement to her, and she wasn't ready for it. He had taken her entirely by surprise with his announcement that he had started the treatment he had been so violently opposed to before, and attributing his change of heart to her. There was silence at her end for a minute, as she thought about it.

"I thought we had something very special when we were together," he said gently, reaching for the moon. It had started with his saving Richard's life, and all the emotions that went with it, as she stood by and watched. It was almost like watching the miracle of birth. He had given Richard his life back, while they waited for reinforcements. They both knew they would never forget it, nor would Richard and Judythe. And now he felt she had done the same for him. It was a bond that joined them, whether she felt ready for it or not. It had happened. He was such good company. There was nothing morbid or pathetic about him, and they'd had fun each time they saw each other. After their earnest conversation, he hadn't looked at his suicide pills since. They almost seemed like an affront now, a reminder of his cowardice. For now, he didn't need them. And maybe with luck, he never would. He intended to go down fighting, not in silence, or taking an easier way out. Gabrielle had given him the courage to live.

"I actually have a lot going on for the next few weeks," she said, feeling anxious, and then guilty as soon as she said it. It wasn't true, and she knew she could make the time to join him, if she wanted to. But that's what she wasn't sure of. Did she want to? Did she need the pain of falling in love with him, becoming close, and then losing him if the disease won in the end? Now she felt cowardly, and guilty for not accepting his invitation. "Let me see what I can do. I'll let you know in a few days."

"It's not an obligation, Gabrielle," he said kindly. "You don't have to come. I won't be angry or disappointed. I don't have the right to expect anything from you, and I don't. I don't even have the right to be starting something with you that could be painful for you in the end. You should only come if you want to have a few fun days in Paris with me. Leave the rest up to me. The treatment is my challenge, not yours, and I don't want to be a burden to you." But he was asking a lot, wanting her to come. He was asking her to live fully again and possibly to love.

"You aren't," she said. "I just need to see if I can change some things around. I'll see what I can do."

"You don't have to do this. We can see each other another time, or not at all if you don't want to. You've already given me the ultimate gift, convincing me to do it. The rest is up to me, the professor, and God. You've done your part. You inspired me to do the right thing. That's huge." He touched her heart with every word, and she wanted to be brave for him, but she needed to think about herself too, and what it would cost her if it went wrong, and it could. He said himself that there was no guarantee the treatment would work. And if it didn't, they already knew the outcome. She wasn't sure she was equal to it, if there was enough of her to help him. She had gone to Paris to celebrate her own rebirth, and newfound strength after Arthur's betrayal, and now this was a much bigger mountain to climb. She felt very small suddenly. But he sounded strong, and equal to what he was doing. He had found the strength he needed. "Tell me what you've been up to," he said, to change the subject to lighter things. "It sounds like you've been busy. How are your girls?" He could tell when she talked about them how much she loved them.

"They're fine," she said, smiling. "Busy. I see so little of them now.

I really miss them. It's so much harder once they grow up. One forgets that they're only on loan. We don't own them."

"I'm sorry now that I never had any. We kept putting it off, probably because we both knew we were married to the wrong person, and then I never remarried. And it's too late now."

"Of course it's not. Arthur was close to your age when we had the girls. And he just had a baby at seventy." She laughed. She could laugh about it now. She hadn't at first. Another of life's great curve balls.

"I'm definitely not ready for that." Alaistair was laughing too. "I can't imagine a baby at my age, let alone seventy." It had never occurred to her when she'd married Arthur, with their twenty-five-year age difference, that he would ever be the one to leave her. She had felt so secure in their marriage, and she'd been wrong. He had suddenly gone berserk, and run off with a girl who was barely more than a child herself, and with questionable intentions. His money had certainly been the lure for Sasha. Gabrielle wondered if she loved him by now, or if she still had her sights set on everything material he could offer her. Gabrielle had no way of knowing and it didn't matter.

They talked for half an hour and she thoroughly enjoyed it. Then Alaistair had to close his office, and she told him again that she would let him know about Paris in a few days.

"I'm not filling the spot with anyone else," he teased her. "You can decide at the last minute. And, Gabrielle, don't make it a bigger decision than it is. It's an invitation to a few days in Paris, that's all. Separate rooms, of course, and it's my treat." It was generous of him, but he felt he owed her at least that for what she had done for him. She had opened his eyes and given him courage. And now he wanted to do something for her. But he had selfish motives too.

Complications

She thought about him that night, and she dreamed about him. In her dream he was dying, and there was a glass window between them, and she couldn't get to him. She could see him suffering and screaming in pain, and she could do nothing to help. There was truth in it, she knew. She thought about it all day, and all night, and for several more days. She wanted to tell him she wasn't coming and couldn't bring herself to do it. It was too big a commitment. But whenever she decided not to go, she felt lonely and sad. She wanted to see him. But she was terrified of getting attached to him and then losing him.

A week after he'd invited her, she called him to say that she'd tried but just couldn't go. She was too busy and couldn't change her appointments. She reminded him that she was coming to an art fair in London in a month and would see him then. He took her refusal with good grace and didn't even sound disappointed. He was a kind man with an elegant spirit. He didn't make her feel guilty at all, which almost made her feel worse. She wanted to go to him, and to see him again, and celebrate and reward his courage, but she was too scared.

He sent her a few funny texts after she declined, and a very funny cartoon by email. He had a dry, British sense of humor, which she enjoyed. He was well-read and intelligent, and had gone to Eton before Cambridge and medical school. It seemed so unfair that she had met someone so remarkable, and good to be with, and he was desperately sick and might not live long. It felt too dangerous to let herself love him, or even be there for him. She felt terrible about not going to Paris to see him, but also relieved.

She wished that she had someone to talk to about it, but she didn't want to involve her daughters in the complications of Alaistair's life, or her own. They were both too young, and the realities were too weighty. They had no life experience with something like it to offer her on the subject, and neither did she. It was one of those knotty decisions she had to face on her own.

She had another bad dream about it three days before she would have gone. And the day before, she woke up in the morning with what felt like a boulder on her heart. No matter what his situation, she missed him and wanted to see him. She hadn't seen him in a month. She sat staring at her breakfast and couldn't eat it, and knew what she wanted to do. She didn't have to sleep with him, or do anything more than she wanted to. She had control of her own destiny, to some extent. It made a lot more sense than Arthur's stupidity with Sasha. If Alaistair died in the end, she'd survive it. Life was about being daring once in a while. She had urged him to be brave, now she wanted to be brave too. She called him ten minutes later. He answered as soon as he saw her name on his phone. He sounded warm when he said hello.

"Can I still come? I've managed to move some things around and I can do it." It wasn't true, but he didn't question it.

"Of course, you can come." And then he sounded serious. "Are you sure you want to? I realized that it's a lot to ask of you. It's a hell of an awkward situation for you. I don't want to burden you."

"You're not burdening me. We'll have fun. Do you feel sick after the treatment?"

"A little rocky the first day, but I was all right the next day last time. It wasn't as bad as I expected. He titered it pretty well. He's very good."

"That's fine. And if you need to, you can stay in bed and sleep. I'll have no problem finding things to do in Paris, especially in that neighborhood." The best shops in Paris were all within a few steps of the hotel.

"I'll call the hotel right away. And, Gabrielle, thank you. It's an incredible gift that you're coming. I've missed you."

"I missed you too. See you the day after tomorrow." Her flight would arrive early in the morning, if she took a night flight from New York. He sounded jubilant when they hung up, and she felt light-hearted all day. She had thought about it carefully, and knew she was doing the right thing. It was what she wanted to do, and she was fully cognizant of the risks. She wasn't walking into it blind. What-ever happened happened, and they'd deal with it.

She rushed to see a client that morning, and came home and packed after that. He had suggested they spend five days there. She got a seat on the flight she wanted, and the following night, she couldn't stop smiling when she checked in. Her fears about going had lifted. She couldn't wait to see him. They would have the week-end together, and he would go for his treatment on Monday morn-ing, and they'd have two more days after that, longer if they needed it. And two weeks after that, she would see him again, in London, when she went to the art fair, but she'd have to work then. Paris was just for them this time, a holiday for her.

She slept on the flight, as she always did, watched a movie, ate a meal, and felt fresh and excited when they landed at Charles de Gaulle. She could hardly sit still, as the car drove her to the hotel. The Louis XVI looked like home when it came into view. In the end, she had booked her own hotel reservation. She didn't want him to pay for it. It didn't feel right to let him do it.

She checked into the hotel at nine A.M., after landing at seven-thirty, and the assistant manager at the desk greeted her pleasantly and welcomed her back. She took her to her familiar room, and five minutes after the bellboy set the bags down, there was a knock at the door. She opened it, and Alaistair stood smiling down at her. He looked thinner and a little pale, but his eyes were bright and he was beaming. He pulled her into his arms and kissed her before she could even close the door to her room.

"Thank you for coming, Gabbie. You're an amazing woman. I don't know where you've been all my life, but thank God I found you." They ordered room service and had breakfast together, while they caught up on each other's minor news.

"I can't believe I'm here." There was an art exhibit they both wanted to see at the Petit Palais. They planned to take a walk in the afternoon, and he wanted to know where she wanted to have dinner. He seemed to have plenty of energy, and despite the slight weight loss, he looked surprisingly well. She didn't press him about his health. They both wanted to spend a happy weekend together, doing fun things before his treatment on Monday. He went back to his room while she showered and changed, and his eyes lit up when he saw her in the red pantsuit she had changed into. It was a glorious, warm, sunny October day, which suited their festive mood.

He had a room next to hers this time. She noticed that there was a connecting door, which was locked. But if they chose to open it, they could. It offered possibilities she had considered for the past few days, and had made no firm decision about. There was no rush to make those decisions. He was letting her make the rules and figure out what she wanted.

"No rock stars in evidence this time," she said with a grin as they left the hotel, remembering when Declan Dragon had destroyed twelve rooms and a suite in the hotel the last time they were there. The rooms were still being redecorated.

"And hopefully no one will have cardiac arrest or get murdered while we're here. There's something I want to do with you this afternoon, by the way," he said, looking serious for a moment, and she looked at him questioningly.

"Something nice?"

"I think so." She wanted to do a little shopping too, but didn't want to bore him. She didn't know how he'd feel about it. They still had much to learn about each other. It felt exciting being with him. They had met exactly a month before, to the day. Everything was still brand new, and she felt young again, as they walked along.

They saw the exhibit at the Petit Palais, and had lunch across the street on the terrace of the Grand Palais, where the Biennale had been held. Afterward, they walked across the Alexandre III Bridge to the Left Bank, and walked along the quais, where the used-book sellers were. They walked down the steps to the river and sat on a bench, watching the Seine drift by, and the Bateaux-Mouches full of tourists. It was a perfect Paris scene, and looked like a postcard. He kissed her, which added to the magic of the moment, and she smiled at him afterward.

"I'm so glad I came. I was scared," she admitted. She felt as though she could say anything to him, and it seemed as though they had known each other for years, not just a month.

"I know you were," he said with an arm around her. "I would have understood if you didn't come. It was a lot to ask. But I'm so glad you did."

"So am I. We'll just take it day by day. We can figure it out as we go along." He nodded, and had come to the same conclusion. He took something out of his pocket after she said it. It was a small pouch and she didn't know what was in it.

"I saved this to do with you." She saw the pouch and was curious. "It's my escape route. I realized that whatever happens, I can't do this to you now. I'm not alone in this anymore. And I can't do it to myself either." He opened it, and she saw three bottles of pills. They were the pills he had gathered and had been saving in case things got too tough. He had removed the labels with the pills inside. "I wanted you to see me throw them away. I don't want them anymore. Hopefully, I won't need them. I'm putting my faith in the professor, and come what may, I will accept whatever happens, and fight till the end." As he said it, he threw the pouch as far as he could into the river, and they watched it float away until it disappeared under the water. When he turned to her, he saw that there were tears sliding down her cheeks and she looked at him gratefully.

"Thank you," she whispered, and then they kissed like all the other young lovers sitting on the benches along the Seine. It was getting chilly by then, and a few minutes later, they got up and walked back to their hotel. They loved walking in Paris and knew the city well. They were both tired when they got back. They'd had a nice day, and his throwing away the pills was deeply symbolic to both of them.

Complications

When she opened her door, she turned and smiled at him. "Do you want to come in for a cup of tea?" she asked, and he smiled.

"I'd love that." He followed her into the suite, and put his arms around her after she closed the door, and suddenly everything they felt for each other, and the decision she had made to come to Paris, overwhelmed them. The tea was forgotten, and they walked into the bedroom of the suite instead, and lay on the bed together. He slowly unraveled her clothes and peeled them away, as she took off his, and they lay naked together. His throwing away the pills he had intended for his suicide was another bond between them. He had chosen life instead, and all because of her. As he began making love to her, he remembered that he had so much to live for, and whatever happened, they would face it together.

Chapter 9

Their second day together in Paris was even more fun than the first. They did a little shopping, went to an auction house, drifted through a number of art galleries on the Left Bank, while they talked about their childhood and families. Alaistair came from a long line of doctors. His grandfather had run a field hospital in France during the war, and his grandmother had been a nurse. Gabrielle and Alaistair were both only children, and their parents had died relatively young. Gabrielle knew that Arthur had been a sort of father substitute for her, after her father died when she was still young. Arthur had betrayed her terribly when he ran off with Sasha. He was chasing his lost youth, and panicking in the face of old age, but knowing that didn't make Gabrielle feel any better.

"I was determined not to let it break me. It came at a bad time, just when the girls were leaving home. I was devastated, but you get over it. I feel sorry for him now. He's stuck with her, and a baby at seventy."

"I just don't want that to be me," Alaistair said. "I missed the boat on that, but I've made my peace with it. The wrong relationships, women hell-bent on their careers. I've always liked strong, independent women, but these days, or in recent decades anyway, most of them don't want children. And I guess I was lazy, and stayed where I was, instead of looking for a girl to have children with. Time moves a lot faster than one expects, and now this. I can still have children, technically, but even if I beat my disease, it wouldn't be fair to have a child. If I had a relapse, or things went wrong, I don't want to leave a wife burdened with bringing up a child alone."

He was an honorable man, and she loved that about him. She had been shocked to discover that Arthur wasn't. His own needs had come first, no matter how great the damage to others, even his daughters. It had been more than disappointing, but she knew who he was now, and their daughters had seen it too. They didn't admire him for abandoning their mother. Gabrielle was young enough that it should have satisfied him. He didn't need to go to extremes with a girl more than forty years younger than he was.

It was all about his ego and the pursuit of youth. His children were embarrassed by how common their stepmother was. No matter how expensive the clothes were that he bought her, some of it haute couture, she always looked cheap or downright vulgar. Georgie said openly that Sasha looked like a hooker, and she wasn't wrong. It had been a terrible blow to their mother, and the girls knew it. They were protective of her now in theory, and their father's remarriage had hurt their relationship with him. But they weren't around to keep Gabrielle company, and she knew she had to learn to live without them. It was written in invisible ink somewhere in the Book of Motherhood. "Thou shalt not hang on to thine children. At the right time, you must let them fly free." She was trying, but it wasn't easy. Nothing would ever take the place of the precious years she had spent with them when they were growing up and still at home. She tried to explain it to Alaistair, and was surprised when he understood. It touched her since he didn't have his own.

"I've always thought that must be the hardest part of parenting. Letting them go. I'm not sure I'd have been good at it. I was in boarding school for years as a boy, and I always remember my mother's face when I went back to Eton after school holidays. She looked as though someone were tearing her heart out. She went to work in my father's office to keep busy, and she did a lot of charity work. She would have much preferred having me at home, driving them mad getting into mischief, and stealing my father's car at every opportunity from the age of fifteen on. I was always madly in love with a girl in the next village." He smiled as he said it, and she laughed.

"You didn't live in London?"

"We did, but we had a house in the country. My parents loved it. We spent weekends there, and summers. In Sussex. I sold it when they died. The place was much too big for me. It didn't make sense for a young man in medical school, and the money was useful. I kept the dower house and a little cottage, and a small piece of land. The dower house was always intended for a widowed mother or mother-in-law. Families stayed together in the days when it was built.

"The manor was quite grand, a big, drafty place with a great hall. My grandfather bought it, and my parents loved it there. They would never have sold it, but times have changed. I'd be lost in the place now, but I always felt guilty about selling it. But the dower house suits me. I go there almost every weekend, and play gentleman farmer. I haven't gone much since I got sick. I'd love you to see it sometime. Maybe when you come to London for the art fair, if you have time. It's quite charming."

She loved the fact that he had a history that mattered to him. He was very English about the land, history, and traditions. He came from a genteel background of landed gentry. They didn't have a title, but there were aristocrats in his bloodline, as he said with a certain amount of embarrassment. "It's all very English, I'm afraid," he said in his modest, self-deprecating way. He saw everything with a tinge of humor, which made difficult things more bearable. Her family had their traditions too. Their family origins were not so dissimilar. Arthur had been a self-made man, which was different. He had less respect for past relatives and family history, and thought them unimportant. It had been a big difference between them.

"We had a summer house on Long Island. I loved going there as a child, but I sold it too. Arthur didn't like it. He wanted something bigger and fancier, so he bought a horse farm in Connecticut. I never liked it, and he kept it in the divorce. But I was always a little sorry too that I didn't keep the house on Long Island. It needed some work when they died, and Arthur didn't want to do it. He liked what was new and shiny, not old with the patina of years and history. That's how he ended up with a flashy young wife, instead of staying with me as I got older," she said with a smile. It was one way to look at it. "I was very hurt by it at first, now I just feel sorry for him. He's stuck with her."

"Which is great luck for me," Alaistair said quickly, and hugged her. "You're hardly 'older,' Gabbie. You're still very young." She was about to turn forty-six, and Alaistair was three years older.

"I have a good hairdresser," she said modestly, and he laughed.

"That's not it. I hate the obsession with youth these days. My worst nightmare would be being with a woman in her twenties. Your ex-husband must be mad. I'd rather like having children, but I would hate to date one. He'll rue the day he indulged that fantasy."

"She'll take the money and run, sooner or later. Women like her don't stick around forever. And there is always a richer man just around the corner in that world. If she finds one, she'll go for it. Or if he starts to slip at some point. He's still active and youthful for his age, but it is what it is. He looks ridiculous with her." She said it in a matter-of-fact way, without bitterness. She had never been bitter so much as bruised by what he'd done. Alaistair was putting balm on old wounds the way he looked at her, with what he said to her, and the way they made love.

He was the first man she had gotten involved with since her ex-husband. She had had some dinner dates, but no one had appealed to her until now. In the give-and-take of life, there was a hitch. It seemed to her that there always was. You got everything you wanted, or almost, and then found that there was something missing. In this case, it was the good health he should have had at his age. It was all a question of what you could live with, and were willing to give up. In Alaistair's case, if they stayed together, and he lived long enough, she'd have to be willing to accept an uncertain future, with a sword over their heads. She was still trying to get used to the idea. But being with him was so easy, and so pleasurable. It was so warm and comfortable and fun when they were together.

It was hard to believe that this was only the second time they'd been together. She felt as though she'd known him forever.

They had seen a small article in the newspaper that morning about the fallen minister of the interior. It said that his trial had been set for January, and that he was being tried for the involuntary homicide of his clandestine male lover and blackmailer. And his crime had been compounded by fleeing the scene of the death.

"This must be awful for his family," Gabrielle commented, when Alaistair had pointed out the article to her at breakfast, since they'd been in the hotel the night it all happened there. There was a photograph of the minister's wife, looking bleak and austere, as she tried to hide her face from the photographer. The brief piece had said that he had a wife and two children.

"Can you imagine the shame of it?" Alaistair said sympathetically. "Look at the poor woman. And why should she be hunted by the press because her husband created this mess?" There was a photograph of Sergei too, from his modeling portfolio, given to the paper by his modeling agency. He looked young and very beautiful, blond with delicate features. The piece mentioned that he was Russian and had come to France with a ballet company, and stayed to become a model. He reminded Gabrielle a little of Sasha, with her high Slavic cheekbones, but he was prettier. "People do some bloody awful things to each other, don't they? And make terrible mistakes. When you think of all he risked. He might have been president of France a year from now, instead he slunk off to a hotel room with that piece of trash, lied to everyone, and brought the roof down on all the people who presumably loved him. I wouldn't want that on my conscience. He must feel like a damn fool now, and rightly so. We so often do the worst harm to ourselves," he said soberly. And for sure, the minister of the interior's career had gone up in flames, and he was likely to end up in prison.

They spent the rest of the day doing things they both enjoyed, and had a delicious dinner at a bistro owned by a famous chef. They were tired when they got back to the hotel, and Gabrielle felt guilty for running him around all day, but he insisted that he'd had fun. They were going to spend the next day taking it easy, before he had his treatment the following morning. From what she could see, he was doing well, considering his condition and the therapy he had started.

They went to bed at midnight, after making love, and she sank into his arms with a happy sigh, and fell asleep instantly. They were both in a deep sleep two hours later, when the phone rang. Gabrielle was afraid it might be one of her daughters, since she had texted them her whereabouts for the weekend. They had assumed that she'd gone to Paris to see a client, or to look at a painting to buy for someone. She was back on the road again, and seemed in much better spirits lately. She had finally recovered from the blow dealt to her by their father. Gabrielle picked up the phone, expecting to hear one of them. It was an unfamiliar voice instead. Alaistair woke up quickly too. He was used to emergency calls at night from his patients. He had left the hotel number with the doctor covering for him.

It was one of the assistant night managers from the front desk, speaking quickly and clearly to Gabrielle in English.

"Mrs. Gates, I'm very sorry, you must leave your room immediately. We've had a credible bomb threat. Don't take time to dress in proper clothes. We must ask you to leave the premises as rapidly as possible. There are police in the hallway to tell you where to go." As he said it, there was a heavy knocking at the door, and she looked at Alaistair as she hung up. She was frightened and wide awake.

"What was it?" he asked her.

She threw back the sheets as she answered him. They were both naked. "We have to get dressed, quickly. There's a bomb threat." Alaistair went to the door to answer it, as she pulled on her nightgown off the floor, and grabbed the terry-cloth robe from a chair. A security person from the hotel was telling Alaistair to vacate the room as quickly as possible. He said they would, and picked up his jeans, which he had tossed on the floor when they went to bed to make love a few hours earlier.

"There's never a dull moment in this place," he said with a grin, and slipped his loafers on without socks, as she grabbed a pair of Chanel ballerinas she had worn that afternoon. "Murder and heart attacks last time, and now this."

Other guests were emerging from their rooms into the hallway, when Alaistair opened the door to their suite two minutes later. They had given up his room after the first night, since they didn't need it. He had moved into hers, since it was bigger and had a living room.

People looked startled and half asleep. It was after two in the morning, and everyone was in nightclothes, hotel robes, or street clothes they had put on hastily. They looked like a motley crew as policemen and security personnel directed people to the stairs on each floor, and they were rushed through the lobby to policemen outside who pointed down the street to a location two blocks away. There were police and SWAT teams all along the way.

Bomb squads were entering the hotel with bomb detection dogs. Olivier Bateau arrived just as Gabrielle and Alaistair were leaving the hotel. He looked as though he had dressed hastily too. He lived nearby. The head assistant manager, Yvonne Philippe, was already there, reassuring guests as they came through the lobby looking frightened and disoriented. They had cleared the bar, and several of the patrons looked drunk as they joined the others heading down the Faubourg Saint-Honoré several blocks to the rue Royale, which was at a safe distance from the hotel. They realized then that all of the buildings on the street had been evacuated, and both the British and American embassies had been cleared as well, as employees and diplomatic personnel got into armored buses and were sped away to another location. A company of marines remained at the American embassy to stand guard, with French gendarmes as well. The British embassy was similarly protected. It was obviously a serious threat, and the French police, SWAT teams, and military personnel were already on the scene.

"Wow," Gabrielle said, as they hurried along and she held Alaistair's hand. She had taken her handbag with her, and he had put his wallet and passport in the pocket of his jeans. It was reassuring to see how many police were on the scene to handle the situation, and a busload of CRS SWAT teams arrived as they got to the rue Royale, as residents of the area and hotel guests milled around in the cool night air. She saw Alaistair shiver and worried if he was warm enough. He was wearing a sweater with his jeans.

"Are you okay?" she asked him, concerned, and he smiled at her.

"My thermostat's been a little off lately from the treatment. I'm fine." She would have offered him her hotel robe, but she would have been standing there in her nightgown, which was transparent. A policeman came by handing out blankets just then, and Gabrielle took two, one for Alaistair and a spare if they needed it, if it got any colder. The church of la Madeleine was at the end of the street, and they were directed toward it, for anyone who wanted to take shelter there, but Alaistair and Gabrielle stayed on the rue Royale. Rumors ran through the crowd like fire, as people guessed at what was happening. No one knew any pertinent details. An hour later, Yvonne Philippe appeared in the crowd, looking for hotel guests she recognized to reassure them. She spotted Alaistair and Gabrielle and spent a few minutes with them. She said she was sure they'd all be back in their rooms soon, and apologized for the inconvenience.

"She should be the manager," Alaistair commented after she left them and moved on. "She's always on deck when something happens. She's young but very efficient. The other guy, Bateau, is a nervous wreck."

"It can't be an easy job," Gabrielle said, not disagreeing with him. "Mr. Lavalle was fantastic until he died, but things are different now. The world is a more dangerous place." There had never been a bomb threat or terrorist at the hotel only a few years before.

More and more people were pouring into the street, and there was almost a festive atmosphere as another bomb squad arrived. People were talking and chatting and wondering what was going to happen. A huge area had been blocked off, and automobile traffic had been stopped. They weren't taking any chances. As the dawn streaked the sky with mauve and pink and orange, police with dogs circulated through the crowd and told people they could return to their homes. A small homemade bomb had been found and disabled. It wouldn't have done as much damage as they feared initially, but they hadn't taken any chances. Alaistair was impressed by how thoroughly the police had reacted, and they slo⟩

in the crowd.

When they got back, coffee, tea, and

the lobby, with stronger drinks being serv⟨

wanted them. Yvonne Philippe greeted the ⟨

in, and Olivier Bateau stood off to the side, wri⟩

guests were good-humored about it, and grateful th⟩   ⟩

protected. Members of the SWAT teams, the gendarn⟩   ⟩d the

military and bomb squad dogs were evident inside and outside the

hotel. It made the guests feel safe to see them, and a surprising num-

ber stopped for a cup of coffee, a pastry, or a brandy on their way

back to their rooms.

"Well, it certainly wasn't boring," Alaistair said good-humoredly,

and Gabrielle laughed.

"This hotel has gotten a lot more exciting than it used to be," she

commented, as they both had a cup of coffee, and Alaistair helped

himself to a chocolate croissant. Everyone seemed to be hungry in

the relief of the moment, and people chatted with one another be-

fore they went back upstairs. The elevators were running again, and

people seemed to feel as though they'd had a grand adventure. The

embassy personnel returned then in the same buses.

But within minutes, people were coming back down to the lobby,

looking puzzled. None of the electronic keys were working and peo-

ple couldn't get back into their rooms. There had been a systems

failure while additional alarms were being activated. Bellmen, office

staff, security people, everyone they could lay hands on had to go

door to door with skeleton keys and open each door manually. The

guests were tired by then and not amused.

..ϲ went to the third floor herself, and let Alaistair ..ιelle into their room with an apology, while Olivier Bateau went to the sixth floor, where members of the Saudi royal family had taken over the entire floor. The whole key system had to be reset and Alaistair smiled at Gabrielle when they finally got back to their room.

"What's next?"

"Hopefully nothing," she said, taking off the robe and climbing into bed, and he slid in next to her. All the guests had to leave their doors unlocked until the key system was rebooted. "If the hotel catches fire, don't tell me. I'm too tired to get up again," she said, as he cuddled up next to her, and they fell asleep.

By seven-thirty, the lobby had been cleared and Olivier went to his office with Yvonne. His hands were shaking and he was pale.

"Christ, it never stops, does it?" he said. He felt sick to his stomach. Yvonne looked calm and in control. "There is always something." The hotel opening started a month before with a dead man in one of their best suites, resulting in one of the most important politicians in France accused of murder, heart attacks, medical emergencies, technology that didn't function properly for an entire month, a destructive rock star, and now a bomb, and all the guests locked out of their rooms. It was way more than Olivier had bargained for when he took the job. "I'm too old for this." He was only forty-one, but his nerves weren't as steady as Yvonne's. She was only thirty-two, nine years younger than he was, but nothing seemed to rock her. She had seemed to know almost every guest by name, as they filtered back through the lobby, and greeted each of them warmly, welcoming them back into the hotel as though it had been nothing more than a fire drill, or a minor event, not a major evacuation of the whole neighborhood. Fortunately, they had found the bomb, although no one had claimed responsibility for it yet. But the police were sure someone would shortly, some extremist group or a lone lunatic. The bomb had been crudely made and had been easy to disarm once they found it, in the basement of a building next door.

"These things happen," Yvonne said to Olivier calmly. "You have to think on your feet and pretend you're not scared." She smiled at him.

"Not scared? I was peeing in my pants," he said with a lopsided grin. "And I'm sure the guests will all be complaining later this morning, and blame us for it, and getting locked out of their rooms. But if we didn't evacuate them and something happened, they'd accuse us of negligence."

"We did just what we should have," Yvonne reassured him. "Some of them looked like they were having fun. At least it happened in the middle of the night, when it was easier to stop traffic, and we didn't have to deal with foot traffic on the street. It could have been worse."

"Yes, they could have blown up the building, or the neighborhood. I'm going to have to write a report for the family." The owners expected reports on everything that happened in the hotel, especially an event like this.

"No one got injured. No one panicked," Yvonne reminded him. They had even provided wheelchairs and people to push them, to evacuate elderly guests. They had thought of everything, and had had several bomb threat drills before they reopened, which had served them well. "And we got everyone out in record time." Even a ninety-four-year-old woman with four French poodles on her lap, barking frantically at the bomb dogs. "I'd say we did a damn good job," she said, and Olivier smiled at her.

"Thank God for you, Yvonne. I'd be lost without you. I think I'll go home now. I'm off today." She was too. There was a competent relief manager for her.

"I think I'll stick around for a while, and make sure there are no medical emergencies, or guests panicking in the aftermath. I have nothing else to do today. And we need to be sure their keys are working again, and no one gets locked in their rooms with another malfunction." He hadn't thought of that. The possibilities for problems were endless. Yvonne was always one step ahead.

He was planning to go home and take a tranquilizer, and she looked steady as a rock, as she poured herself another cup of coffee from the machine in his office. "You can go home. I'll be here." She had no other life than this hotel. It was her opportunity of a lifetime, and she was willing to sacrifice everything for it. A personal life and a job like this simply weren't compatible, unless you put your own needs second after the hotel's. Their guests had to be the first priority for management at all times, even on their days off. Yvonne was fully aware of it and willing to accommodate.

"My father ran a hospital in Bordeaux, and died of a stroke at fifty-seven," Olivier told her. "I think it killed him. This place is going to kill me if things don't calm down," he said unhappily.

"They won't," she assured him. "Working in a hotel is like being a fireman, you have to be prepared for the worst at all times." She loved it, she lived and breathed everything that happened there. He could see it, and he envied her. And he hoped she was wrong, and it would settle down to a dull roar soon. They had just been unlucky so far. "Go home. Don't worry. I'll be here."

He left gratefully a few minutes later, and took a tranquilizer for his nerves before he left. Yvonne went to make rounds of the hotel to make sure that the employees were on point, doing their jobs as efficiently as always, and not slacking off after the emergency. The relief manager took over the desk, while she took her tour of the hotel. She found most of the staff functioning well, and a few who were smoking in the basement halls in small groups, which was strictly not allowed. She reprimanded them. It had to be business as usual for them. They couldn't afford the luxury of either panicking or relaxing. She went back to her office, changed into a simple navy-blue dress and high heels, and braced herself for the day. She didn't need the Sunday off anyway. She had no one to spend it with. The hotel was her lover, her husband, her family, her best friend, her baby, and the place on earth that she enjoyed most. The guests were the children she'd probably never have and didn't care. This was enough for her. She went to the front desk then, and remained visible to any guest coming through the lobby. She greeted each of them, and they felt better once they saw her face. She watched all of it with an eagle eye, the guests, the employees, and she had a bag of lollipops for the children, which she handed out with their parents' permission, and treats for their dogs. Seeing their faces, content to be at the Louis XVI, was reward enough for her. She was always surprised by the big tips some of the guests gave her. She didn't do it for that. She did it out of love for the hotel and the people they served. She had no family life. Her father worked for an oil company in Saudi Arabia and her mother was dead. Her sister lived in India, and her brother worked on an oil rig. She had grown up all over the world. And the Louis XVI was her home and her family now.

Alaistair and Gabrielle woke up at noon after a long nap. They ordered breakfast and were talking about what had happened, and how efficiently it had been handled both by the hotel and the police.

"I like this hotel," Alaistair said with an arm around Gabrielle. "They do a good job, and they take good care of us." She nodded agreement, closed her eyes, and nestled against him. She was still tired after the four and a half hours they had spent on the street, with only two hours of sleep under their belt before that. And she'd been afraid of what would happen if the bomb went off. But it all seemed unreal and like a movie now when they thought about it.

They dressed and went out after they ate, walked for a while, and then came back to the hotel when it started to rain. It was a fine drizzly mist, and it was cozy being back at the hotel. She wanted him to rest before his treatment the next day. They watched movies on the television in the room, and ordered dinner from room service. Their room keys were working again and there was no evidence of the night before.

"Thank you for being here with me," he said gratefully, as he smiled at her over their dinner. He would have taken her out, but she insisted on staying in. It was raining harder, and cold, and she wanted him to be in optimum condition for his treatment the next day. He had a moment of anxiety after they ate, and looked depressed and pensive.

"Are you worried about tomorrow?" she asked him gently.

"Not the actual treatment," he said sadly. "I can manage that. It's about what comes after that. I have no right to drag you into this with me, Gabbie. The odds are terrible, and if I don't beat them, I'm leading you down a path you don't deserve. Watching someone you care about die, losing someone you love. If I was a responsible person, I'd end it with you now. But apparently, I'm not," he said somberly. "This isn't fair to you."

"I'm an adult, Alaistair. You've been honest with me. It's my choice to be here. And we don't know what will happen. You're in treatment now, with one of the best researchers in the world. You may win this fight. And if you do, do you really want to throw this away on the chance you won't? Life is complicated. Love is messy. There are no guarantees. I could be hit by a truck. I could be sick instead of you. Hopefully, we'll be able to put this behind us. You have to fight for your recovery. And I want to be with you, whatever happens." She was in now. She wasn't afraid to be anymore.

"You hardly know me. Why take the risk?"

"Because this was given to us. We found each other. It's a gift, and you never know what's going to happen next. Richard almost died, and you and the other doctors saved him. He has his life back. They didn't even know he had a problem. Now he and Judythe have a future. I'm not giving this back, or running away from the risks. Amazing things happen, both good and bad. This is what we have to face now. I'm willing. I thought about it a lot before I got on the plane to come here. I'm not here by accident, or blindly, or because I had nothing else to do. I'm here by choice. You're a miracle in my life. A year ago, I thought my life was over. Now it's beginning again. I'm not going to run away from that, or from you, because it's complicated. If we weren't facing this, we'd be facing something else. I'm in.

You're not going to scare me away. And if the worst happens, we'll have had all this before it. I'm not giving that up. Other than my children, you're the best thing that ever happened to me." He was smiling again. She had known all the right things to say, and he could see that she meant them. He had felt so guilty before that.

"What if I turn out to be a shit? You don't know me yet."

"I know enough. And if you turn out to be a shit, I'll come here with some twenty-two-year-old cabana boy and tell him what a jerk you were. How's that? I'm not giving up on you, Alaistair, whatever you say. Now shut up and eat your dinner, so we can go to bed and make love. Or shouldn't we do that before your treatment tomorrow?" She looked worried and he shook his head.

"They never said anything about it. This is France. I think we can make love whenever we want." He was smiling and she laughed.

"Good." She grinned at him, and then came to sit on his lap, and shortly after, they wound up in bed. He still felt a little guilty for dragging her into the fight with him, but so blessed and lucky to have her with him. She was a brave woman, and he loved her.

An hour later, as they drifted off to sleep in each other's arms, peaceful and sated, and grateful that they had found each other somehow in the midst of their respective battles for survival, Yvonne Philippe was just leaving the hotel and going home. She had been at the desk since the bomb threat the night before. She had worked twenty hours straight on her day off. She put on her coat, and left through the employees' entrance after signing out.

She'd had a good day, exactly the kind of day she'd expect to have, with a full house, the day after a bomb threat that had unsettled everyone, on a Sunday that was supposed to be peaceful and never really was. The German baroness's dachshund had swallowed a chicken bone and needed to be rushed to a vet, the SAMU had to be called when a little girl couldn't breathe from a seafood allergy they hadn't known about. The eighteen-year-old son of a Saudi prince had crashed his Ferrari and needed a doctor for a gash on his arm. Three televisions had broken and had to be replaced. The main chef had threatened a sous chef with a knife. And a six-year-old girl from Cleveland had lost her favorite doll, and Yvonne and her mother had gone through five trucks of hotel laundry and found it. Her mother gave Yvonne a three-hundred-dollar tip, but she hadn't done it for the money. She didn't have the time off to spend what she made.

It had been a good day. Yvonne walked down the street thinking about it, and hated to leave the hotel for the night. Something would happen, someone would need her. But they could always call her and she'd come back. There was nowhere else she wanted to be. It was the one place in the world where she felt happy and needed and safe. No matter what happened there she knew she could handle it with enough patience and love and ingenuity and courage. What else was there in life? Nothing else mattered to her except the Louis XVI and their guests.

Chapter 10

On Monday morning, Alaistair and Gabrielle got up at seven o'clock. She had set her alarm, and had the hotel operator call them to be sure. She woke up before the alarm, and took a shower before Alaistair stirred. She touched him gently and he smiled at her the moment he saw her face.

"I'm awake," he said sleepily.

"So, the snoring was an act?" she teased him. "Incredibly convincing. You've got it down to a fine art." He got up then, and she ordered a light breakfast for them, although she was too nervous to eat, and he wasn't supposed to eat more than a light meal before the treatment.

They had agreed the night before that he would go on his own, and call her when he was ready to be picked up that afternoon. They were going to keep him for several hours to make sure that there was no untoward reaction to the drugs. There hadn't been last time but that could change. The professor wanted to observe him himself, and if necessary, Alaistair could spend the night. He was in essence a research subject, but far from the first patient to have this protocol for the same illness. The disease itself was rare, but the professor had treated a number of cases from all over Europe. It was his passion.

Alaistair left the room at eight-thirty looking serious and distracted, gave Gabrielle a hug, and assured her that everything would be fine. He hoped so himself, and was somewhat anxious, but didn't want to frighten her. She appeared calm when he left and told him to have a good day in school and behave himself with the other kids, and he laughed. After he left, she sat in a chair in the living room of the suite, staring into space and thinking about him.

She had paperwork with her to do for her clients, but it was hard to concentrate. She got very little done, and she started looking at her watch at four o'clock, hoping to hear from him soon. By five o'clock she was worried, but she didn't want to call him, in case he was still in treatment, or not feeling well. She didn't know what to expect. She was trying not to panic, when she heard the door open ten minutes later, and Alaistair walked in. He looked tired, as though he had a long, exhausting day, but he smiled as soon as he saw her.

"Why didn't you call me? I was going to pick you up."

"The professor drove me home. We seem to have hit it off. He has a reputation for being taciturn and unfriendly, but I think he likes the fact that I'm a doctor. He dropped me off. I'm the only clinical patient he has right now, so I get special treatment." He sat down in a chair across from her, and he seemed worn out, which wasn't surprising. The drugs he was given to kill the cancer were very powerful, but he seemed to be weathering it well. The doctor had told him he was lucky. "How was your day?" he asked her, wanting to make the day seem more normal, and to hear about whatever she did.

"I thought about you, and I did some paperwork. How did it go?"

"Astonishingly well. The professor is very pleased, but this is only the second treatment of the big guns, with one middle-of-the-month cocktail in London," which was milder but also necessary. "We won't know anything for a while. He thinks you're an effective part of why I'm doing well. He says the spirit is very important. If you can cure the spirit, often you can heal the disease, or chase it off for a while. Our goal for now is remission, not a cure. That can come later, with new developments. I'd settle for remission. Step by step," he said with a sigh.

"So would I," she said, and came over to kiss him. "Do you want something to drink?" She was thinking of tea or fruit juice or even water.

"Something tall and cold would be great. I'm dying of thirst. I couldn't eat or drink all day. But I'm not hungry."

"I had a great lemonade this afternoon," she suggested, and he nodded gratefully.

"Perfect." She ordered it, and it arrived ten minutes later with a plate of thin butter cookies, which he ate and drained the glass. "Do you mind if I sleep for a bit? I'll be better tomorrow." He went to bed and she tucked him in and saw the bandage on his arm from the IV and didn't comment. He was asleep within minutes, and didn't wake until midnight. She checked on him regularly, and had time to think again of what she had stepped into. She knew the risks she had taken, and the responsibility she had assumed, to stand by him, and accept him, whatever the outcome in the end. She had no regrets, and was glad she had come.

He was hungry when he woke up at midnight. She ordered him boiled eggs and toast, which was all he wanted, and he went back to sleep as soon as he ate it, and woke up at eight o'clock the next morning. He had slept for fourteen hours and obviously needed it. He seemed surprisingly normal in the morning, he ate a big breakfast and wanted to go out with her. They went for a walk along the river, and stood under a tree to avoid the rain.

"Thank you for doing this with me," he said gratefully. "It's a lot to ask of anyone."

"You didn't ask. I volunteered. I enlisted," she reminded him.

"Thank you." It was their last day together, they were both leaving in the morning, but she was going to London in two weeks for the Frieze art fair, and to be with him. He was going to have his mid-month treatment then. He said it was less draining than the one in Paris, which he would have again in a month. She had already started reorganizing her schedule, without telling him, so she could come back to Paris with him in a month for the next treatment there. And they were going to go to his dower house in Sussex when she came to London, after his treatment and the art fair. She had invited him to go to several of the events at the fair with her, and he was looking forward to it. Just as she was to seeing his house in Sussex.

He was still a little tired from the day before, and they took a cab back to the hotel, where he took a nap. But that evening he insisted on taking her out for a nice dinner. They went to a well-known restaurant, and he ate well. And when they got back to the hotel, he looked like himself again. He had recovered rapidly from the treatment. It seemed less rugged than she had feared, but he was a strong man and not given to complaining. She was impressed by how brave he was, and said so.

"I'm a doctor. I'm supposed to know about these things. I urge others to do them, so I can't very well whinge myself."

"Yes, you can. You can do whatever you want."

"Besides, I need to be in form for my patients. I'm damn lucky, I've found a good locum tenens," which she knew now was a relief person for a doctor, "who can give me the time I need to come to Paris for the treatments, and he gives me a day for my mid-month cocktail, and here and there when I need it. He's a good man, and a cancer survivor himself. So, he's quite sympathetic. He's got a smashing Jamaican wife and four very cute kids. He's one of the lucky ones. He's a ten-year survivor now. His kids are all very young. He froze his sperm before the surgery, sorry for the details. She went through it all with him. You'd like her. The marriage caused quite a stir in his family. His father is in the House of Lords, very old name, an earl. He's a viscount, although he doesn't use it. They're an amazing couple, and his family has finally come around, but it was rough for them for quite a while, between his parents and the cancer. I'm not sure which was worse. At least we don't have that to deal with." He smiled at her. "Are you going to tell your daughters about us?" he asked her, and took her by surprise. She'd thought of it, but it was much too soon. They'd been through enough with their father and his Russian bride.

"Eventually. Not yet."

"I'd like to meet them when you think the time is right."

"They'll like you, but I don't want them to worry that I'm going to run off and leave them. I don't see them much, but they like knowing that I'm in one place waiting for them. It doesn't occur to kids, even at their age, that parents need their own lives."

He smiled at what she said. "I can see that. I was always very annoyed when my parents had their own plans that interfered with mine, or went on holiday without me. It seemed incredibly selfish of them." He laughed at the memory. "I don't think you really appreciate your parents until they're gone." She nodded, agreeing with him.

"I didn't, until I had kids of my own. And then it's too late most of the time. They're off to their own lives somewhere else."

They spent an easy, relaxed evening, and went back to the hotel. Gabrielle had already packed, and she helped him pack when they got to the hotel. They had a last loving night together.

In the morning, he argued with her about who would pay for the room, since he had given up his, and wanted to pay the bill for hers, and had offered to when he invited her to Paris. But it was a very expensive suite and she insisted. She paid for it in the end, and he said that the next trip, if she came to Paris for the next treatment, was on him. She was planning to stay with him in London. He had paid for everything else on the trip, and was a generous man.

He left before she did, to catch the Eurostar, since he was seeing patients that day. He said he felt up to it, although she thought he still seemed tired. The professor had called the evening before to see how he was, and was satisfied with what Alaistair reported to him.

They had a hard time leaving each other, and saying goodbye. She wasn't used to parting from him yet, and felt an ache of loss as soon as he had left. He called her when he got to the train and checked in, and a few minutes later, she left to catch her flight to New York. It had been a wonderful five days. They had stretched it to have the time together, and his relief doctor in London was willing and needed the money. He had six mouths to feed. He had a title but very little money, so the arrangement suited them both. She felt as though she had already lived half a lifetime with him, what they were going through was so intense, with his illness and the treatment and the uncertainty of the results. She felt like she was falling through space with him, and couldn't see the ground beneath them yet or where they would land. It was an odd feeling, but everything else about it was right.

She slept on the flight and arrived in New York at two P.M. local time. After going through customs, she was home at four P.M. Veronica called her from L.A. almost as soon as she walked in.

"How was Paris?" she asked, and Gabrielle thought of Alaistair as soon as she said it. She had called him from the cab to tell him she'd arrived safely, and he had just gotten home after a long day of patients, and told her he missed her.

She felt dreamy when she answered her daughter's question. "It was wonderful." Veronica didn't suspect anything. She had no reason to. "And we had a bit of excitement. There was a bomb scare and we spent four hours on the street in the middle of the night."

"How scary! Was it okay?"

"Yes. They found it in a basement next to the hotel and disarmed it in time."

"That's so dangerous, Mom. Maybe you shouldn't go to Paris anymore."

"It can happen anywhere these days. But the police were amazing. They were all over the place."

"Well, be careful. I'm glad you're back in New York."

Gabrielle tried to reach Georgie that night too, but didn't get her. She was always busy, out, with friends, and never picked up her phone. She only communicated by text, and Gabrielle preferred hearing her voice.

And at nine o'clock that night, trying not to go to bed too early, so she could get on New York time, she answered the phone and it was Judythe. She sounded jubilant and excited.

"We wanted you to be the first to know. We're getting married in December. We hope you can come. We're going to invite Alaistair too. We were going to wait until spring, but we kind of got a jump start on things," she said, sounding mildly embarrassed. "I just found out I'm pregnant. It must have happened in Paris that night. The baby is due in June, and I want to get married before it shows." She said it all in a rush, and Gabrielle smiled. They had almost lost everything, and now they had an abundance of riches. They had each other, a baby, and were getting married. They had been richly rewarded for everything they'd been through to finally be together. They couldn't ask for more. They had wanted to start a family, and Gabrielle remembered that Judythe was thirty-nine.

"That's wonderful! Alaistair will be thrilled when he hears. I just saw him in Paris. I got home a few hours ago. This is great news. And I will definitely be there."

"I haven't organized it yet, but I'll let you know the date as soon as I book a room. We only want a few people there. We both had big weddings before. Once is enough," she said, laughing, and Gabrielle was happy at their news. "We wouldn't be getting married if Alaistair hadn't saved him." But Judythe would have had his baby to console her at least, if her guess about when it was conceived was correct. But now she had them both, Richard and their child.

"I'll tell Alaistair when I talk to him," she promised, and was still smiling when they hung up. It was one of those sweet moments that made everyone feel good. A total win-win, which touched and blessed them all. She was happy Judythe had called. And she had reported that Richard was doing great, and his doctor in New York said he was fine. The episode in Paris had saved his life, by putting a spotlight on a problem they hadn't even known existed and would have killed him if it hadn't been repaired and the defective valve replaced.

The two weeks Gabrielle spent in New York flew by, seeing clients, bidding in an important Sotheby's auction, making plans with dealers she wanted to see in London while she was there. In the blink of an eye, she felt like she was packing again.

She planned it to arrive the night before Alaistair's mid-month treatment in London, and this time she drove him and picked him up, very cautiously driving on what was the "wrong" side of the road for her. Alaistair let her drive his car. She met Geoffrey Mount Westerley, Alaistair's locum tenens, and found him delightful. They stopped in at Alaistair's office in Harley Street on their way back from the treatment, and then went back to his place so he could sleep.

He had a loft apartment with a view of the Thames. They had to climb a ladder to get to his bedroom, but it was a perfect bachelor pad, and suited him. He slept late the day after the treatment, and after he woke up, they decided to drive to Sussex for the weekend.

She was excited about going there with him, and the art fair didn't start until Monday, so they had the weekend together, with no other plans. They'd originally planned to go to Sussex after the art fair, but he couldn't wait to show it to her. And he felt well enough to go and rest there.

It was a beautiful fall morning when they arrived in Sussex, and he parked his hunter green vintage MG outside the dower house. It was a beautiful home with graceful proportions, which would have been adequate on its own, with a small guesthouse beside it. And she could see the grandeur of the manor house in the distance through the trees, with a lake and swans on it between the main house and the dower house. It was a magnificent property, and was a symbol of a bygone era of great elegance and wealth. She could see why he hadn't kept the manor for himself though, when he'd inherited it as a young man. The manor house was huge, and would have required an army of servants to run it, which was what his family had when his grandfather bought it from a family that had lost their money.

The grounds were beautifully maintained, and she followed him into the dower house, which was cozy and warm, with wood-paneled rooms, and the beautiful antiques he had saved from his parents' home. It was in sharp contrast to his modern loft in the city. His house in the country looked like a miniature ancestral home, which was what it had been when his great-grandmother lived there. Alaistair had added a number of masculine touches, including a den filled with comfortable oversized leather chairs in front of a large fireplace with a black marble mantel. There were several ancestral portraits, including two handsome ones of his parents, one hanging in the living room and the other in the front hall. He had antique hunting prints in the den. The whole house looked very British and very distinguished. Gabrielle felt instantly at home there, and told him how beautiful it was.

"I'm so glad you like it." He looked pleased, as he led her up to his bedroom to set down their bags. There was a big antique four-poster bed made of carved mahogany. "I couldn't bring myself to give all this up. I grew up with it, and the new owners didn't want it. They redid the whole house and it's very modern. This is all very old-fashioned, but it's familiar and I love it." And Gabrielle did too. He had dark Persian carpets that wouldn't show if you brought mud in from outdoors, oversized leather furniture, and dark green velvet upholstery and drapes. It had a masculine touch, but she felt at home there too. "This is where I spend all my weekends. My ex-wife hated it, but the place means a lot to me. I always feel at peace here. It's like crawling back into the womb. It reminds me of my parents and my childhood, and our family history." Gabrielle could see why he loved it. It was a beautiful home.

They had bought groceries before they left London, and made lunch in the big old-fashioned kitchen. And afterward, they went for a long walk around the property and came back to admire the swans on the lake. It was a peaceful place, and she relaxed just being there. All the strains of the day were forgotten. Alaistair put an arm around her as they sat on a bench and watched the graceful, elegant birds glide by, with a few ducks swimming along the edge.

"I haven't brought anyone here in a long time," he said quietly. "I like being here alone. Or I always did. Now I like being here with you." Being there made his illness seem unreal, and all their daily concerns. It made their questions about the future seem unimportant. The property and the houses on it had been there for so long that it gave one a sense of permanence and the reassurance that it would always be there. It was a place to calm one's fears, and they walked back to the dower house together hand in hand. They didn't say anything to each other, they didn't need to. Then they went up to his bedroom and made love. There was an overwhelming sense of peace about the place, and Gabrielle lay in Alaistair's arms for a long time, wishing him long life and health, and hoping that she would be there to share it with him. She could almost feel his ancestors who had lived there before, blessing them, and wishing them well.

They cooked dinner together that night. And the most modern thing in the house was a large television in the den, where he watched sports and movies. They picked a film together, and watched it. And then they went back to bed. It was a blissfully simple life.

They went riding together the next day, over the hills. The new owners allowed him to ride some of the horses in their stables. It gave Gabrielle a feeling of the size and grandeur of the property as they saw it on horseback, and went past the farms, which had once been tenants of his grandfather, in the old days. Now they were rented out, and a few had been sold. They were used as country homes by Londoners more than farms. The whole scene was so picturesque, Gabrielle wanted to stay there forever. It was a magnificent property, and selling it when he had had allowed it to be preserved by people who could afford to run it well.

"They're not here often. They live in South Africa," he explained to her. "They intend to retire here one day, or so they say. I'm not sure they ever will, they have a number of beautiful homes, but at least they keep it up, and they love it. I'm happy I still own a tiny piece of the property and can come here."

"I'm so glad I've seen it." It was an important part of him, and a glimpse into who he was, and where he had grown up. The original owners had been one of the great families of England, who had eventually lost their property and money over the generations, but at least it was still intact, and no one had bought it to turn it into a hotel, or cut it up in small lots for a development. So many old estates had been destroyed or simply disappeared.

They went to bed early again that night, and got up early the next morning. Alaistair did some gardening after breakfast, which he enjoyed, and Gabrielle read a book. They had to tear themselves away when they left on Sunday night to return to London.

"I don't think I could leave if I lived here." She smiled at him.

"I have a hard time leaving it myself." And he was obviously pleased that she loved it so much and understood it.

They were both sad when they got back to his flat in London, and she had a busy day ahead the next day at the art fair. He was going to join her there on Tuesday night, after he finished seeing his patients.

"I'm so glad I saw the dower house," she said, as they climbed into bed that night. "When can we go back?"

"Whenever you're here." He smiled happily. "I'm always happy to spend time there." He remembered as he said it the battle it had been to get his wife to go there, until finally she refused. She missed the excitement and pace of London, and her friends. She didn't understand British country life, it wasn't bred into her as it was in him.

They lay in his comfortable bed that night, side by side, snuggling under the comforter, and she fell asleep, wishing she could stay in London longer, and had more free time while she was there. But she had a business to run, clients to satisfy, and she had less than a week in London to do everything on her agenda. Being with Alaistair had a fairy-tale quality to it, but like it or not, now she had to go to work. And he did too. Real life was nipping at their heels, with all its delights and terrors.

Chapter 11

Alaistair left to go to his office when Gabrielle went to the art fair, and he joined her there at the end of the day. They both enjoyed it, even more than they had the Biennale. There were many galleries represented that Gabrielle did business with regularly, and the art was particularly good that year. Speaking the language made it easier for her, even though the galleries represented both in London and in Paris were from all over the world, Europe, Asia, and North and South America. It was a world-class event, and Alaistair thoroughly enjoyed following her around, and meeting the people she introduced him to. He found her life fascinating. It was a much more sophisticated world than his as an internist, but she was interested in his work too. Their time together was full of new discoveries and shared experiences. He found that being with her gave him strength, and it did the same for her. She didn't feel as though she had to fight every battle alone anymore. In an unspoken way, in a short time, they had become best friends and allies. And beyond that, they were fighting for his life. They tried not to focus on that all the time, and to lead a normal life. They had dinner one night with some of his friends. They were excited to meet Gabrielle. And one of them, an old classmate of his, was an artist, and she particularly enjoyed meeting him.

The week she had planned to spend in London ended too quickly. She had to meet with a few clients that weekend and they couldn't get back to Sussex.

"Duty calls," she said, but she had promised to meet him in Paris again for his next treatment with Professor Leblanc at the beginning of November. They were going to run some tests then to see what effect it was having. It was too early to expect drastic results, but the professor was hoping to see at least some small improvement. Although he didn't like admitting it to her, Alaistair was nervous about it. What if it hadn't worked at all? What if the numbers were worse? He didn't dare put words to all his fears, but she could sense that he was stressed about it. Since he hadn't felt ill to begin with, it was hard to gauge any improvement now. He felt well and in good spirits when he was with Gabrielle, and most of the time, except the day of a treatment or the day after when he was exhausted from the chemicals and poisons being injected into him to kill the cancer. But none of it was as unpleasant as he had feared it would be. It all seemed to be happening underground, where he couldn't assess what was happening or if anything had changed.

With great sadness, he drove Gabrielle to the airport on Sunday night. He kissed her when they got to the airport and he pulled up at the curb. "I'm going to miss you awfully," he said sadly.

"Me too. But I'll see you in Paris in two weeks," she reminded him.

"You're becoming quite the jet-setter," he teased her. She wasn't going to stay with him as long in Paris next time, since she had to get back to New York to work and organize Thanksgiving. And as she thought about it, she turned to him with a question.

"Do you want to come to New York for Thanksgiving and meet my girls?" It was a bold move on her part and she didn't know how Georgie and Veronica would react. And her relationship with Alaistair was still very new. But by Thanksgiving, they would have been seeing each other for almost three months. And it might be the right time to meet her daughters, since they were spending Christmas with their father, and Alaistair wouldn't get another chance to meet them anytime soon.

He looked pleased when she asked him, but hesitant. "Are you sure?"

"Yes, I am," she said firmly. She suddenly loved the idea.

"What if they hate me?"

"We'll spank them and send them to bed without dinner. No turkey for them." She would never have done anything like it, even when they were small, but he laughed and it relieved the tension.

"I guess that's fair enough. And yes, I'd love to come. I just don't want to upset them."

"I'll give them fair warning so they get used to the idea." And if they objected really violently, she could always explain it to him and change plans. She didn't want to get off on the wrong foot with them. They were a powerful force in her life, and he knew it from everything she said about them.

He kissed her again, carried her bag to the check-in counter at the curb, and left her with a wave as he drove away. She wished she was going with him. She worried about him, and at other times she forgot and had to remind herself that he had an illness. He seemed so well, but they both knew that there was an evil demon lurking in the shadows, waiting to destroy them, or destroy him, and break her heart in the process. But it was easy to hide from it sometimes when he was in good form, which he was much of the time.

They had fun plans ahead. She had already told him that she wouldn't be able to come to Paris for his December treatment. She would be too busy in New York after Thanksgiving. In the first week in December, she was going to the Art Basel fair in Miami. It was an extraordinary event, and she had invited him to go with her. He was planning to fly over and meet her there for a long weekend after his treatment in Paris. She would have meetings with several clients and many art dealers at the fair. He had never been there. That and its sister show in Basel, Switzerland, every summer were the two most important art fairs in the world, and Alaistair was excited to see this one. He had heard about it but never been to it. She was enriching his life immeasurably. After the art fair in Miami, they were flying back to New York for Richard and Judythe's wedding. Then he was flying back to London. Gabrielle was going to spend a few days with her daughters to celebrate an early Christmas before they flew to the Caribbean with their father.

Before she left, Gabrielle had accepted Alaistair's invitation to join him in Sussex for Christmas, so she wouldn't be alone after all. With all their plans, they were going to be flying a zigzag course across the Atlantic for the next two months. But as long as he felt well enough, and they could both afford to, there was no reason not to. She had never expected this to happen, but once she had decided to seize the moment, with her initial trip to Paris, the opportunities to do fun things and spend time with him had rained down on her. It reminded her that not only bad things happened, but also good ones. There was often a random pain floating somewhere in a life, or a price to pay, or an added heartbreak. In this case Alaistair's illness. But that wasn't slowing him down, and she was grateful. For the moment, he was on borrowed time and they both knew it.

Gabrielle was so busy in New York after the London art fair that she barely had time to talk to him. The invitation to Richard and Judythe's wedding had come, and she and Alaistair both accepted. They wouldn't have missed it.

It felt like only days since she'd seen him, when she got on a plane and flew to Paris to meet him for his next treatment at the beginning of November. They had a day together before, to enjoy Paris. She waited for him at the hotel again while he went for the treatment and had a battery of tests. He looked more tired than the last time when he came back to the hotel.

"I think the man is a bloody vampire." He complained to Gabrielle about the many blood tests the professor had done. And as he had before, he slept again until midnight. But the next day he was in better form this time, and they had the weekend to spend together. The weather had turned cold in early November, and they were starting to put up the lights for Christmas on the Champs Élysées and the avenue Montaigne, and in the neighborhoods. She could see how beautiful it was going to be for Christmas, and she was sorry she wouldn't be there to see it, since she wasn't coming back for his next

179

treatment. She knew he could manage without her. She was just there as moral support, but he was comfortable doing it on his own too. It was a much shorter trip for him on the Eurostar than it was for her from New York. He didn't expect her to be there every time, but he was grateful when she was.

They had an exceptionally good white truffle dinner at Alain Ducasse, and they had lunch at their favorite bistros and ate hachis parmentier, a dish of duck and mashed potatoes, smothered in black truffles. They walked for miles, looked at the shops on the Faubourg Saint-Honoré, already decorated for Christmas, and made love as soon as he felt better after the treatment.

It was going to be very different from the last two Christmases for her, still mourning her marriage then, and not yet back in the swing of things. Now she felt alive again. She and Alaistair laughed and talked, and went dancing on Saturday night after dinner at a small disco Alaistair knew from his youth and student days. It was still there.

They left the hotel together on Sunday morning, in separate cars, she to the airport, and he to the train station to take the Eurostar back to London.

They had talked endlessly about his meeting her daughters on Thanksgiving. He was terrified of doing or saying the wrong thing. "Girls are tough," he said warily. "If they hate me, they'll convince you not to see me again."

"I have a mind of my own, you know," she reassured him. "They're not going to convince me of anything. And besides, they won't hate you. They're too busy hating their father's wife. There is nothing objectionable about you. Will you please relax?" It was all they talked about now, which at least distracted them from worrying about the results of his recent tests. Professor Leblanc had said that they wouldn't have the results for a week, maybe two.

Gabrielle had two weeks to catch up on her work and get ready for Thanksgiving when she got back from Paris. Time was speeding by, especially with all the traveling she was doing, and September and October were already a blur, except for meeting him. Like an infant that was almost three months old, it was hard to remember now a time when he wasn't in her life. She told him about her days, and her work, her clients, and her concerns about her daughters. It was more of a partnership than she'd had with Arthur. Arthur had always made the rules and dictated what they did, and for a long time had treated her like a child, not an adult. It was probably part of the appeal with Sasha. But one day she would grow up too. He wanted the women he loved to stay children forever so he could control them. She hadn't realized that was what he did until after he left. She finally under-stood that he would have left her sooner or later, even without Sasha. Gabrielle had grown up and become too independent. She had de-veloped her own opinions and ideas, which wasn't what he wanted in a woman. He wanted someone he could mold and control. Gabri-elle was no longer that person. She realized now that their marriage had been doomed anyway as a result. It wasn't entirely Sasha's fault.

It was also why he quarreled more with their daughters now. They had strong opinions too, as they grew up. They had judged him harshly for leaving their mother, and were critical of his choice of new wife. He had already warned them to be nice to her during their holiday in Saint Barts. He had chartered a yacht, and the girls were excited about it. Sasha was too, and had bought a whole new wardrobe for the trip. They were bringing the baby and the nannies. It was a three-hundred-foot motor yacht. Arthur never did anything small. Gabrielle was surprised that she didn't miss that about him. She wanted a smaller life now, more human scale, ordinary pleasures. Her trips to Paris staying at the Louis XVI were luxurious enough, she didn't need more luxury than that in her life. A three-hundred-foot yacht would have been fun, but having that in exchange for opinions of her own, or a voice in their marriage, no longer seemed like a good trade to her.

The week before Thanksgiving, she landed an important new client, Dmitri Spiros. He owned a shipping line. He was Greek and had a four-hundred-foot yacht he sailed into New York Harbor, and anchored at the dock of one of the cruise lines. He had been referred by one of Gabrielle's clients in London. He wanted her to help him buy all the art for the boat, and had a heavy preference for Picasso. It would take months, and her commission would be sizable. The boat was brand new. She toured it with him, took photographs and made notes of all the places where he wanted paintings and sculptures. He was a man in his sixties, he wasn't handsome but he had an interesting, heavily lined face, and she noticed that he had a very young girl with him. She was French and in her early twenties. It made her wonder why men like him always had very young women, and never a woman whom they could talk to, who would genuinely contribute to their life. They took the easy out, and preferred a young girl as a kind of decoration, even though they knew why she was there, and that she wouldn't stay forever. Men like him preferred to buy their women, just as Arthur had with Sasha. They were a special breed. She had been twenty-one and Arthur forty-six when they married.

And this time he was seventy with a twenty-six-year-old. It seemed pathetic to Gabrielle now. She much preferred her relationship with Alaistair, who had less money, was less important in the world, had a more normal career, listened to what she had to say, and treated her as an equal. That was a first for her. All Arthur wanted was a decoration, like a tinsel angel on the top of the Christmas tree, sparkling and pretty.

She enjoyed the day she spent with her new client on his yacht, and told Alaistair all about it when she got home. She told the girls about it too, when they called, and at the end of the conversation, she told them that she had invited a friend to Thanksgiving.

"What kind of friend?" Veronica asked her, sounding suspicious. She knew that her mother had had very little social life since her parents had separated. She was embarrassed by Arthur leaving her at first, and then seemed to have outgrown most of their old friends. She was hoping to make new ones, but had only just emerged from her cocoon in the past few months. She said that her metamorphosis from caterpillar to butterfly wasn't complete yet, but she was working on it, and finding her way.

"He's a friend I met in Paris a few months ago. He's a doctor, and he lives in London." There was a long silence while Veronica digested the information.

"Are you dating him?" Long pause again while Gabrielle decided what to say, and concluded that the truth was simplest. If her daughters wanted to be adults now, she had a right to be too.

"Yes, I am."

"Is it serious?"

"I don't know yet." She didn't tell her that he was sick, and might not be around long enough to be a problem, although she hoped he would be. "He's a nice person, and we enjoy each other's company. We're both going to a wedding in New York after Thanksgiving, and I thought you might like to meet him."

"Is this what it's going to be like from now on, Mom? We have to spend holidays with Dad's gold digger and your dates?"

Gabrielle didn't like the comment but could understand why she was upset. Arthur had forced Sasha on them, and she had lorded it over them ever since. Sasha had their father's ear and frequently complained about them.

"He's not Sasha. He's a nice man."

"Does Georgie know?"

"I told you first. If it really upsets you, he doesn't have to come. He's English, so Thanksgiving isn't a big deal to him. He just wanted to meet you because I talk about the two of you a lot. And he'll be in New York anyway for that wedding."

"I guess it's okay." They had had big Thanksgiving meals with many friends when she and Arthur were married, and now it was just the three of them. He had invited friends on the boat he'd chartered over Christmas, so they wouldn't get time alone with their father.

Life was a party to Arthur, so he could show off his child bride. He liked having people envy him, and most of the people around him did. Gabrielle had realized after he left her that if she met him now, she wouldn't be interested in him, or maybe even like him. But he had dazzled her as a young girl. He'd been fatally handsome and attentive. He had wooed her and swept her off her feet. Now they had nothing in common, except their two girls. Gabrielle's world was smaller now, and she preferred it that way. Alaistair's dower house in Sussex was much more her cup of tea. She wanted a real life, not the superficial one she'd had with Arthur.

Gabrielle called her younger daughter after they hung up. Georgie didn't seem to care if Alaistair came to Thanksgiving or not. She was busy with her own life, and in a hurry on the phone.

"Whatever you want, Mom. Is he cute?"

"Cute enough," her mother said with a smile. She thought he was handsome, but didn't want to admit it to Georgie.

"Can I bring someone too?" The question startled her mother, and caught her off-guard.

"Who did you have in mind?" She hadn't thought of it being a quid pro quo, but it might ease the tension for Alaistair and help break the ice.

"I've been going out with someone here. He's from New York. He's going home for Thanksgiving, but his parents don't make a big deal of it. You'd like him."

"Okay. Does he own proper clothes or will he show up in sweats and Nikes?" Her friends usually did. Veronica was meticulous about the way she dressed, and had a grown-up job at the museum in L.A. Georgie still dressed like she was twelve, and going to a basketball game in the park. "And that applies to you too," she reminded her.

"I know, I know. His dad is a lawyer, and his mom is always dressed up when she comes to visit here, so I know he has decent clothes somewhere. Does he have to wear a tie?" She sounded worried at that.

"No, but a jacket would be nice if he owns one, and real shoes." Gabrielle was a stickler for dressing nicely for holidays, and she set a beautiful table.

"Mom! What about black high-tops?"

"Whatever." Gabrielle had relaxed her rules over the years. She was just happy to see them, and have them home, whatever they wore. "You'd better take decent clothes with you though, to wear on the boat. Your father won't want you wearing flip-flops and shorts to dinner."

"I know, Mom," she said, sounding exasperated. "The princess wears gold lamé to breakfast. Dad must be going blind. Or getting senile. He loves it." Gabrielle didn't comment, but she smiled, listening to her daughter. "See you in a week, Mom. I don't have classes on Wednesday, so I'll be home Tuesday night."

"I can't wait to see you." Veronica was coming home Tuesday too. And they were staying until Sunday. She loved having time with them.

Gabrielle just hoped, when she hung up, that everyone would get along, and they didn't give Alaistair a hard time. They were very possessive of her now that she was alone, and she had come to realize that they liked her that way. They didn't see why she should have a man in her life. They hadn't been that way before, but in their minds, she belonged to them, and even if they weren't around anymore, they intended to keep her that way. It was easier for them if she was alone.

* * *

Complications

Alaistair landed in New York on Monday night, which gave them twenty-four hours together before her daughters arrived. She had invited him to stay with her, so he came from the airport by cab, and she was waiting for him at the apartment. It was already midnight in London by then, so she assumed he wouldn't want to go out. She had a light dinner for him of cold cuts and smoked salmon, and some soup. He was moving to the Mark hotel the next day before the girls landed. Her apartment was on Seventy-fourth Street and Fifth Avenue, so his hotel was only four blocks away. It was a popular hotel with a good restaurant. After the girls left, she and Alaistair were leaving for Miami and Art Basel. They planned to be there all week, and then fly back to New York for Richard and Judythe's wedding, the weekend after Thanksgiving, Alaistair was flying to Paris Monday after the wedding for his treatment. And she was flying to London to meet him after the girls left for St. Barts. It was going to be a very full few weeks. When they came back from Miami, he was going to stay with her again. The girls would be gone by then. She didn't want her daughters to know that, it would put too much weight on their meeting, which Gabrielle wanted to keep as light as possible. His staying with her would be a big message to them that this was serious. They didn't need to know that yet.

Alaistair looked tired but thrilled to see her the minute he walked into her duplex apartment. He admired the view of Central Park. It looked like a Christmas card with snow on the ground. He was impressed, but not surprised, by the art on the walls. She had some very handsome paintings, some by unknown artists, others by some very big names. They had been left to Gabrielle by her father. Much of their important art had belonged to Arthur since he'd bought it, and he had taken it when he left. Gabrielle didn't miss it. Alaistair liked the paintings she had. She was wearing jeans and a pink sweater, and he smiled as he followed her into the kitchen, leaving his bag in the front hall. He sat down at the kitchen table, while she set the food down in front of him. She had set the table with pretty linens, and a bunch of white flowers. He leaned over and kissed her when she joined him.

"You can tell that a woman lives here," he said, and she raised an eyebrow.

"Really? Why?"

"Everything is so neat. Men are genetically incapable of achieving that effect," he said, and she laughed.

"You're pretty neat too."

"Only when I'm expecting a visit from you," he confessed, and she laughed again.

"You could be right. I like a tidy house." She noticed that his hands were shaking then. Not extremely but slightly. He saw her watching, as he helped himself to a piece of the salmon and a lemon. She didn't ask him about it.

"It's a side effect from the drugs," he answered her unspoken question. "And headaches at times, and occasional dizziness and weakness. Things are heating up. The battle rages on," he said, making light of it, but he had felt the effects of the last treatment in November more than before. "But the good news is it seems to be working. Professor Leblanc called this morning, before I left with the results of the last blood tests. The numbers are better. Not a lot, but the needle moved a little. He thinks it's a good sign. He's going to increase the dose when I go back, and really blast me for the last three rounds. The cocktail in London is stronger too. I hope your daughters don't notice the shaking hands and think I'm a drunk."

"It's not that noticeable. I just look closely." But he looked all right. Better than when she'd left him two weeks before.

She showed him the apartment after he ate. It was beautiful, and very different from his London loft. Her apartment was airy and light, the lighting was soft, with a spectacular view of the park from both floors. There was a roof garden, but all the plants were dead, from the cold weather and the snow. She had it replanted every spring with bright colored flowers.

At the end of the tour, they wound up in her bedroom. She had debated about sleeping there with him. She had never slept in that room with anyone other than Arthur, and thought it might bother her, or Alaistair, but in the end, she decided to stop treating the room like a shrine. She had made room for his clothes in a closet, and pointed to Arthur's old bathroom across from hers. It was an elegant apartment. The girls had grown up there, and had kept their rooms. It was still home to them.

He unpacked what he needed for that night while she watched, and he went to take a shower. He came back with a towel wrapped around his waist, and she smiled when she saw him. He looked sexy and young for his age. He had a beautiful body, and she gently tugged the towel away, and he kissed her. A few minutes later, they were in the bed she had shared with Arthur, and the ghosts were exorcised forever. The memories of Arthur faded into the past.

Their future was uncertain, but the present, bathed in love and joy, was enough for both of them.

Chapter 12

They took a long walk in Central Park the next morning, and had lunch at the Mark hotel, after they moved him in. And after lunch, they walked down Fifth Avenue past all the shops, until they got to Saint Patrick's Cathedral, and went in. It was a magnificent church across from Rockefeller Center. The giant Christmas tree was in place, but it hadn't been lit yet. Gabrielle lit a candle for each of her daughters and a big novena candle for Alaistair.

"Who's the big one for?" he whispered to her gently after she opened her eyes and sat back on the pew next to him.

"You," she said solemnly, and he smiled.

"That's probably better than Professor Leblanc's treatment, and it won't make my hands shake," he whispered, and she leaned over and kissed his cheek.

They walked back uptown all the way to his hotel, and christened the bed there, and they lay close together afterward, her long dark hair spilling over him, until she thought she should leave. She wanted to be dressed and waiting when the girls arrived. She was having dinner with them at home that night. Alaistair was going to have room service and watch a movie. He admitted to being exhausted. He was jet-lagged and after the five miles they'd walked that day, he felt like he deserved a lazy night in his hotel room. She wanted him to drop by the next day to meet the girls. She hoped to catch them before they went out to see their friends. All of Georgie's friends would be home from college for the long weekend. Many of Veronica's had dispersed to other cities, Chicago, Boston, Houston, Miami. They had jobs all over the country now, and she loved hers in L.A.

"People stay closer to home in England," he commented. "Most of them can't afford to move to other cities, unless their jobs pay for it."

"I wish that was true here. I love it when they're home." He could see the longing in her eyes and how much she missed them. A little while later, she left to walk back to her apartment. She had everything ready for the girls by the time Veronica arrived from the airport. Her room was fresh and aired, the bed was made with clean sheets, and there was something to eat in the fridge if they wanted it. They never did. All they wanted was to go out and see their friends. Georgie's room was ready for her too. Gabrielle made sure that everything was perfect for them when they came home.

Veronica gave her an enormous hug, and then checked her phone to see who had called. She was texting her friends when Georgie walked in half an hour later. The house came alive when they were there.

The two sisters left together twenty minutes later. Georgie said that all her friends had arrived and she was going to visit two or

Complications

three of them. Veronica's very best high school friend, Julie, was home too, for the weekend. So, the house was empty again, but it was nice knowing they'd be home to spend the night. She loved catching glimpses of them, as they flew past her, and she loved seeing them in the kitchen when she got up in the morning.

She called Alaistair to say good night after the girls had left, and he was already half asleep, watching TV.

"I miss you," he said groggily. "How are the girls?"

"Out, predictably. They'll be back later. I'd come over to visit you, but I'd fall asleep on your bed and never make it back." They had gotten spoiled with the nights they spent together, and the trips they had shared.

She heard the girls come in later that night, and was making coffee when they got up in the morning. Veronica already had plans for the day, and Georgie was texting all her friends on WhatsApp. Gabrielle could already guess that they had everything set for the day, and she texted Alaistair to come by at noon, so she could introduce him before they left.

They were ready to leave but hadn't gone out yet when he came by. They looked startled when the doorbell rang and their mother walked into the kitchen with a man. He was tall and good-looking, with blue eyes and gray hair. They had forgotten about Alaistair in the midst of contacting their friends, and looked surprised when their mother introduced them. Catching them by surprise made them shy and took them a little off balance, which Gabrielle had decided was a good thing. Georgie was the first to recover, and looked him over with interest.

"Are you the mystery guest for Thanksgiving?" She grinned at him.

"I believe I am," he said, as Veronica joined them, not to be out-done by her younger sister. "I came from London for a turkey dinner. I've never had a real Thanksgiving. And I came to meet you as well. Thank you for letting me join you," he said politely.

"I'm bringing a friend too," Georgie said casually. She was wearing jeans, combat boots, a pea coat, and a beanie, and looked very cute. "He's buying shoes today, or Mom wouldn't let him through the front door. So, don't show up in Nikes," she warned Alaistair, and he laughed.

"I brought Adidas," he said, and she grinned. He was friendly and nice.

"Mom says you're a doctor," Veronica said. She looked chic in a red coat she had bought in L.A., and she was wearing black heels. It looked to her mother like she had a date, but she clearly didn't in-tend to tell them. She didn't have a boyfriend at the moment that they knew of.

"I am," he answered Veronica's question. "I'm an internist."

"That's actually how we met," their mother explained. "When I went to Paris in September. We were both staying at the Louis XVI. I opened my door, and the man in the room across from me had had cardiac arrest. Alaistair was giving him CPR. He saved him." She thought she'd give him some extra points with the story, and both girls looked impressed.

"I gave him CPR, but a whole medical team called the SAMU, and a surgeon, saved him. I just kept him going till they got there. It was pretty dramatic. He was only thirty-eight years old."

"That must have been scary," Georgie said, impressed, and even

Veronica looked interested. She liked the way he talked to them, and noticed the warmth in his eyes when he glanced at their mother.

"He had an undiagnosed heart anomaly, which could easily have killed him. But he had surgery that night, and he's fine now."

"That's pretty heroic. Did he thank you?" Georgie asked him.

"Yes. He and his fiancée invited me to their wedding. And your mother, too. It was actually a very unusual evening. Someone got murdered a little while later, down the hall."

"Murdered?" Veronica looked horrified. "You mean like shot? Or stabbed? Were other people killed?"

"No. They're saying now that it was an accident. It was some kind of dispute between a gay politician and a blackmailer, and one of them died in the process."

"Maybe you should change hotels, Mom," Veronica said to her, and she smiled in answer.

"It did occur to me, but your father and I always liked this one, and it's in a great location. No one else got hurt." She didn't tell them about the bomb scare or they'd never let her go back to Paris. "Declan Dragon was staying there too. He trashed a whole floor of the hotel, and they threw him out." Georgie looked fascinated by the information and Veronica was smiling as she picked up her handbag to go out. She glanced at Alaistair. He didn't seem like a major threat to either of them, and he had handled the introduction well. Both girls left in the next three minutes and Georgie reminded him to wear proper shoes to lunch the next day. He said he would. He let out a long breath when he sat down at the kitchen table after they'd left.

"Now, that wasn't so bad, was it?" Gabrielle asked him, and leaned down to kiss him.

"I just pretended they were new patients and kept up the chatter," he said with a smile.

"Your bedside manner is excellent. You charmed them both. I know my daughters. You'll get free passage tomorrow. I'm glad you met them today. Now they can see that meeting you is a non-event. You didn't gush over them, and treated them like ordinary people."

"They're very pretty girls," he complimented her. "They look like you."

"Veronica looks like her father. But Georgie looks like me at her age. She just has more self-confidence. Nothing fazes her."

"I was a nervous wreck about meeting them," he admitted, but she knew it anyway. "I'm not used to girls their age. But they're not scary. They're very polite and poised. I can imagine them giving their Russian stepmother a hard time though." They were smooth, intelligent, well-educated girls, and it showed.

"Arthur got off on the wrong foot with them, and sprung his new wife on them. That never works with them. And she's a lot to deal with. They'll be fine with you now. Mysteries don't go over well. And a surprise like Sasha was a real shock to them." But there was nothing shocking about Alaistair. He was a gentleman and a kind, warm person.

They spent the afternoon shopping and doing errands. Alaistair went back to the hotel to rest. Both girls told her when they got home that they had dinner plans with friends. She picked up Alaistair at the hotel, and they went to a neighborhood restaurant and had a good dinner. Then Alaistair walked her back to her apartment.

She invited him upstairs for a drink, and he said he was too tired, and after he kissed her, he went back to his hotel. She was glad they had gotten the introductions over with. The girls seemed to have no objection to him. If they had, they would have pulled their mother aside then and there and told her. They had treated him like an unnecessary accessory, but not the enemy. So they had gotten that far without major incident. Gabrielle knew that Alaistair was going to sleep much better that night, no longer worried about meeting them. And the next day was Thanksgiving. They were all looking forward to it.

When Georgie's friend showed up the next day before Thanksgiving lunch, he was wearing brand-new black leather size-fourteen oxfords that looked more than respectable, but he hadn't gotten the memo about hair. He had dreadlocks that made him look like a porcupine, and a bull ring in his nose that almost made Gabrielle gasp when she saw him, and she overheard Georgie whisper to him in the hallway, "I told you not to wear it to lunch." But he did anyway. He was a bright, interesting boy, a political science major at George Washington University. He was wearing black jeans with holes in the knees, a wrinkled plaid shirt hanging outside his pants, and a mustard-colored corduroy jacket that was three sizes too small. He could barely move in it, and he said it belonged to his younger brother who was in eighth grade. He said he had a blazer but couldn't find it, and thought his mother might have given it away.

His name was Joel, and his family lived in Tribeca, which was trendy, but he clearly didn't own anything decent to wear, contrary to Georgie's assumptions. He was a nice kid, and helped get lunch on the table, and Gabrielle didn't say a word to Georgie about him. There was no point. Georgie was wearing a black mini skirt and knee-high Doc Martens with fishnet stockings, and a black sweater, and Veronica was wearing a pale gray Chanel suit of her mother's and black high heels, similar to what her mother was wearing. Alaistair showed up in a dark gray suit, a white shirt, and navy-blue Hermès tie. Gabrielle thought he looked very handsome.

The turkey came out just right, and Gabrielle told him how to slice it. The girls had helped her with the gravy and vegetables, and Gabrielle had made two kinds of stuffing, with chestnuts and without. It was the perfect Thanksgiving meal, and they had an array of pies for dessert, apple, mince, pecan, and pumpkin, with whipped cream and vanilla ice cream. They were all too full to move at the end of the meal, but they had loved it. Alaistair was impressed by Gabrielle's cooking skills.

"Don't be. It's the only meal I know how to make decently. I make it on Christmas, too. I'm not known for my cooking."

Joel left shortly after lunch, and three of Georgie's girlfriends showed up to hang out in her bedroom. Veronica left with a date, who picked her up downstairs to go to someone else's Thanksgiving dinner, and Alaistair and Gabrielle sat in the living room, talking. There were mountains of dishes in the kitchen, waiting for the housekeeper the next day. It had been a fabulous meal, and everyone was happy. Alaistair had enjoyed getting to know Gabrielle's two daughters and the conversation had been lively, with girls their age. They had talked about politics, fashion, and asked Alaistair if he had kids.

They seemed relieved when he said he didn't. Veronica talked about the museum, and Georgie talked about a paper she was writing.

"I like Thanksgiving," he said warmly.

"It's a nice excuse to get everyone home," Gabrielle said to him, and they both laughed about Joel's outfit and his bull ring. She was less amused by his hair. "If we all get lice from his dreadlocks, I'm going to kill her for inviting him," Gabrielle commented.

"You won't get them unless you wear his hat." He had put the whole thing in a reggae hat when he left, and thanked Gabrielle very politely for the meal. He said he had to get home to have another dinner with his parents and brother. "I guess he had to give him back his jacket," Alaistair said to Gabrielle. He had been exploding out of it all through lunch and could barely move his arms. "It's fun having them around," Alaistair said to her with an admiring look. "You manage it well."

"There's not much to manage. They're all grown up, or almost. Georgie has to finish school, they need to pick careers they love, and hopefully they won't marry someone who looks like Joel." She summed it all up and he laughed.

"He was very polite," Alaistair said with a grin. "And very bright. I thought you handled it very gracefully. I wasn't sure what you were going to do when I saw the bull ring."

"I decided it wasn't worth getting excited about. I don't think she's in love with him, or she won't be for long. She was more excited about seeing her girlfriends. I think she just invited him because I invited you, not to be outdone. Her father gets upset about what she wears. She'll outgrow it."

"I would have been a terrible father. I would have focused on all the wrong things."

"As long as no one's on drugs, pregnant, or in jail, I can live with the rest," although she kept a watchful eye on all of it.

"My parents were tyrants about my grades," he volunteered.

"The girls were both good students, so I didn't have too much to worry about there. Now I worry about the big stuff, like their marrying the wrong guy one day. But hopefully, that's still a long way off. I was younger than Veronica when I married Arthur." She smiled at Alaistair. "Thank you for coming. At least you know my children now."

"I hope I get to see more of them."

"So do I," she said softly.

Once the girls were gone, she went back to his hotel with him, and they lay on his bed. It had been a long day, and it was nice to be alone. He fell asleep as she lay next to him, and she watched him, hoping that Professor Leblanc's treatment was working magic in his body. She gently smoothed his hair and left him sleeping peacefully after a while to go home and be there when her daughters came back. It had been nice having him with them. It somehow made it all seem more real. He was no longer a secret.

Veronica said something to her about it when she came in, while Gabrielle was trying to make a semblance of order in the kitchen, and had changed into jeans.

Veronica grabbed a bottle of water to take to her room. "I like your friend, Mom," she said quietly.

"Thank you. So do I. He's a good person. It's a little complicated having him live in London and me here." Veronica nodded. It seemed complicated to her too, but things had a way of working out, if they were right.

"It's easier that he doesn't have kids. It's hard meeting other people's kids. It's just one more complication," Veronica said innocently.

But instead of kids, he had a fatal illness and was fighting for his life. At least he was fighting and hadn't given up. She thought about the pills he had thrown away in the Seine.

"I'm sorry we're leaving you alone for Christmas, to be with Dad and the step-monster."

Gabrielle smiled. "I'll be okay."

And Veronica could see that she would be. She seemed happy these days, and not just because she had a man in her life. She seemed to be enjoying herself and was at peace.

"Will you be with him on Christmas?" Veronica asked her.

"I think so," she answered. Veronica nodded and went to her room. Things were different than they were when her parents were together, but at least their mother was better now. After Veronica went to her room, Gabrielle turned out the lights in the kitchen, and prayed that it wouldn't be Alaistair's last Christmas. That would be so unfair. But if it was, they would make it the best Christmas of his life, and she'd remember it forever. It was what they had for now. And all they could do was live it day by day.

Chapter 13

W hen the girls left on Sunday to go back to L.A. and Washington, D.C., after Thanksgiving, Alaistair moved back into the apartment with Gabrielle. She and the girls had had brunch together that morning, and Alaistair had joined them, and the girls hugged him when they left. The gesture surprised him, but he was touched.

"Take care of my mom," Veronica whispered to him, and he nodded. He had tears in his eyes when he turned away. Taking care of her was all he wanted to do, and he hoped that the Fates would allow that to happen. Their future was a mystery that neither of them could foresee. But who ever could? He had an arm around Gabrielle's shoulders when the girls left. He only wished he had found her sooner, but the time they were sharing was infinitely sweet.

They flew to Miami on Monday, and Gabrielle had made reservations at the Edition, which was a convenient place to stay to have access to the fair. There were smaller satellite fairs in addition to Art Basel. She was meeting three clients there, and looking for pieces for four others. It was a heavy workweek for her, in a fascinating place for him. They dropped their bags off at the hotel, and went straight to the main hall, where some of the booths were still being set up. She liked being there at the beginning, before the best pieces sold. She told Alaistair it would be a madhouse in a few days, and she had easy access everywhere with passes the dealers had given her. Seeing it with her was exciting and an adventure for him. When she met with one of her clients, Alaistair went back to the hotel to sit by the pool. He was tired these days, more than he wanted to admit, the repeated treatments were taking a toll. He never admitted it to Gabrielle, but she knew. She encouraged him to sleep late and relax when he could. It was a wearing event for anyone, but even more so for him.

He spent two days at the fair with her, and then explored Miami, and sat by the pool. The warm air and sunshine felt good. He was checking in with Geoff regularly in his office, and everything seemed to be going smoothly there.

By Friday, Gabrielle had seen everyone she needed to see, and accomplished what she had to do. She'd bought some terrific pieces for her Greek client with the yacht, including a fabulous Picasso. The sale was handled in the strictest confidentiality, and she had bought it without disclosing who the client was. She told Alaistair all about it, and she fell asleep with her head on his shoulder on the flight to New York. There was a light flurry of snow falling when they landed, and it was late when they got home to her apartment. Central Park already looked like Christmas, dusted with snow.

They slept late the next day, and dressed for Richard and Judythe's wedding. It was being held at the Plaza at six o'clock. There was snow on the ground and it was bitter cold. There were about thirty people gathered, and Alaistair and Gabrielle were honored to be among them. Judythe looked exquisite in a pale lavender gown, holding violets, with her blond hair loosely piled on her head. And Richard looked handsome in a dark suit, with a sprig of violets on his lapel.

Judythe's parents were there, and her ninety-year-old grandmother. The ceremony was performed by a minister, and they both cried when they exchanged their vows. They had fought hard to get where they were, and it had taken time. They were thrilled about the baby she was carrying. It barely showed, and Richard looked at her as though he couldn't believe how lucky he was. In his wedding speech, he attributed his even being there to Alaistair and Judythe for keeping him alive in Paris until the SAMU came. Gabrielle squeezed Alaistair's hand when he said it. Without that whole episode, she might never have met him at the hotel. And now Richard was healthy and alive, he and Judythe were married, and a baby was on the way.

They were flying to Rome for their honeymoon just as they'd planned. It was a happy ending and beginning beyond all their dreams. It felt like the perfect wedding to celebrate it.

Alaistair and Gabrielle spent Sunday together the next day, and on Monday, Alaistair flew to Paris for his next treatment. Gabrielle stayed in New York. She had work to do for her clients after Art Basel, shipments to confirm, wire transfers to handle. The girls were coming back to New York for an early Christmas celebration with her, before flying to Saint Barts on their father's plane to meet the boat he had chartered. She had a busy few weeks ahead of her, and on the twenty-third, she was flying to London to spend Christmas with Alaistair. They were going to spend it in Sussex at the dower house, which sounded perfect to her.

Alaistair called her when he arrived in Paris. He was staying at a small hotel on the Left Bank this time, closer to the professor's office. He wasn't planning to stay long. Just one night, to sleep off the effects of the treatment, and then he was going to take the Eurostar home to London.

The professor was satisfied with the results of the tests from Alaistair's last visit, and he wasn't surprised by the weight loss and fatigue he was experiencing. It was what he expected at this point in the treatment. Alaistair was halfway through it. And after this session, there would be two more, in January and February, and then they would see what long-term benefits he got from it, if any. He had already lived a month past what was expected when he started. They hadn't thought he would live past November then. Every day was a gift now, and the future was a mystery that remained to be discovered.

He felt worse than usual when he got back to the hotel where he was staying, and he was too tired to even text Gabrielle. When she didn't hear from him, she wondered if he had bad news and didn't want to tell her. He woke with a start at two in the morning, and called her. It was only eight o'clock at night for her, and she had been worried sick about him when he didn't call her. Tears filled her eyes when she heard his voice.

"Are you all right? What did he say?"

"He said I'm doing fine. The side effects don't surprise him. But I was so tired when I got back to the room that I fell asleep with my phone in my hand while I was texting you. I'm so sorry. I didn't mean to worry you." He could hear that she was crying, and hated that he was the cause of it. He had dragged her into it with him. And there might be worse to come, and a tragedy in the end. But it was too late to turn back now. They were in it together. She had joined him knowingly, and they had to ride the waves now until the end, wherever it took them.

"I was so worried when I didn't hear from you."

"I won't do that again, I promise."

"I'll be there soon," she said in a soft voice, wiping her eyes. "Don't worry about me. I'm fine," she reassured him. "I'm just tired. Miami always wears me out. Just go home tomorrow and rest. Why don't you have Geoff stay for a few extra days?"

"I'll be fine," he assured her. "I can't make Geoff work all the time, although my patients seem to love him. He's such a sweet guy."

"So are you, and I love you. So, behave yourself. And wear your mask on the train, so you don't catch anything." She had made him wear it on the flight to Miami, and he felt stupid wearing it, but Professor Leblanc had suggested it too. Contagion was his enemy in his weakened state. His immune system was almost nonexistent now.

He went back to sleep after they talked, and caught the train the next morning. He slept all the way to London. When he turned up at his office, Geoff sent him home. He looked exhausted, and Geoff told him he'd scare the patients if he stayed. He had dark circles under his eyes, and an unhealthy pallor that had worried Gabrielle for the past month. But he seemed to be holding up in spite of it.

* * *

The girls arrived in New York the week before Christmas to spend the night with their mother, and exchange gifts. She knew all the things they liked, and she made their traditional turkey dinner, but substituted a chicken, which was the right size since there were only three of them. They said a tearful goodbye when they left and apologized again. They were both relieved that she was flying to London to see Alaistair and wouldn't be alone. She reminded them not to be disagreeable to Sasha, or it would put their father in a bad mood and he'd be angry at them. They knew she was right, but they both found Sasha unbearable. She'd be showing off on the boat, and cooing at their father. It was going to be a real challenge not to lose their patience with her. And the baby cried all the time. They were going to do their best to avoid Sasha, and fortunately, the boat was enormous. The two girls left arm in arm, and felt terrible leaving their mother, and said they wouldn't do it again.

Gabrielle took the flight to London the night of December twenty-second, and arrived as promised on the twenty-third. She found Alaistair in bed, even thinner than before, and Geoff had been covering for him for several days.

"Should we call Professor Leblanc?" she asked Alaistair. He had been warned that when the end came, it might be fast, and he was on overtime now from their original prognosis. He was following the professor's protocol, but he looked like he was dying anyway.

"I already did call him," he told her. "He says this is all to be expected. He ran tests again, and the results were good enough. He says it gets harder toward the end of the treatment, and we'll know more in January and February." He'd had his mid-month "cocktail" in London the week before, and it had hit him hard this time. She packed his bag for Sussex, and he drove, but he was so exhausted she was afraid he'd fall asleep at the wheel. She kept him awake talking to him, and trying to make him laugh, giving him the girls' first reports of the boat trip with Sasha. When they got to Sussex, Gabrielle put him straight to bed in the huge mahogany four-poster. She brought him some soup a little while later that they'd brought with them, and he was already sound asleep, so she didn't wake him, and took the soup back to the kitchen. She just hoped he wasn't dying and they didn't know it. But Geoff had told her there was a hospital nearby, and if she had to, she'd drive him there, although she didn't like driving on the wrong side of the road at night. But she would have done anything for him. She was grateful to be there with him.

She lay down next to Alaistair without disturbing him. She lay there for a long time, watching him breathe. He looked so peaceful, it frightened her. But he woke up in the morning feeling better. She had barely slept all night, while keeping a watchful eye on him. He ate a decent breakfast, they went for a short walk afterward, and he looked more human again. He could see that she was scared. She was wondering if it was a good idea to be there, and if they shouldn't be in the city closer to his doctors.

"I'm fine," he insisted. He took a nap after lunch, and they made a fire that night. It was Christmas Eve, and they sat holding hands until almost midnight. And then they went upstairs to bed. He looked peaceful and happy, as he lay smiling at her.

"You're the most beautiful woman I've ever seen," he told her.

"Now I know you're going blind," she said, and he laughed.

"I'm not blind, and you're crazy for being here with me. I hope I can make it up to you one day. We should go somewhere when this is all over." It was the first time he had spoken of the future and wanted to make plans. She didn't know if it was some kind of delusion, or if he really felt he was getting better, or was trying to cheer her. "Merry Christmas, by the way."

"Be a good boy and go to sleep, or Santa will put reindeer poop in your stocking." He laughed, and a few minutes later he was asleep. In the morning, he actually looked better, and felt stronger than he had in days. She didn't know if it was a sign that the end was coming or if it was genuine improvement. She had heard that sometimes people got a surge of energy right before the end.

The girls called her that morning to wish her a merry Christmas, and they were having fun, in spite of Sasha, who was wearing a rhinestone thong and going topless on the boat, and their father loved it. Georgie told her mother that he was losing his mind, or had when he married her. Gabrielle didn't comment. She didn't want to add fuel to the fire of their hatred of her.

After they called, she and Alaistair exchanged gifts. She had bought him gold cuff links because he wore them to work every day. She'd had them engraved with his initials. And he had bought her a diamond band ring, which he slipped on her finger and it fit perfectly. He put it on the finger where she'd worn her wedding ring and she smiled when she saw it sparkling there, and made no objection to the meaningful gesture.

"When this is all over, I'll make that legal if you like. In the meantime, you can wear it, waiting for better days." She smiled again and kissed him. It was an extravagant gift and she loved it.

* * *

They spent a week in Sussex, and he got slightly better every day. They were both dreading his next treatment in Paris, which would weaken him again. Alaistair had called the professor, and he said he was going to put him in the hospital for the day for the next one, and possibly keep him overnight.

They went back to London on New Year's Day, and hated to leave the peace and warmth of the dower house. And the day after their return to London, they took the train to Paris, and checked into the Louis XVI.

"If anyone commits murder this time, it'll be me, if they have another bomb scare," he said. He was irritable, worrying about the treatment the next day. She took him to the hospital and stayed with him until the professor entered the room to administer the treatment. They sedated him, which they hadn't done before. He slept the day away, and they kept him overnight. But he didn't seem quite as weak as he usually was afterward. He only had one more treatment to do, in a month. And they had gotten him through this one, which was the most powerful dose so far.

They stayed at the hotel for two days, and when they got back to London, he was well enough to go to his office, which was a vast improvement. Gabrielle was living on her nerves now, constantly worrying about what would come next, but the stronger treatment hadn't hit him as hard this time. Gabrielle flew to New York at the end of the week. She had to meet her Greek client, and was going with him to install his new Picasso on the boat. He had brought the yacht back to New York for the installation of the Picasso and five other new paintings she had bought him.

When Gabrielle left London, she told Alaistair she would come back at a moment's notice if he needed her. If he didn't, she had several weeks of work waiting for her in New York, and she was going to meet him in Paris for the last treatment, and all the tests Professor Leblanc wanted to do at the end of his therapy. For now, they had gotten through the holidays, and he was still alive. It felt like a major victory to both of them.

There had been some nights when she hadn't dared to sleep at all. She was wearing his ring when she left. She hadn't taken it off since he'd given it to her, and he wore his new cuff links on his first day back at the office. Geoff had noticed them immediately and complimented him on them. He was relieved to see Alaistair looking better. He had turned a corner somewhere between Christmas and the New Year, and was getting his strength back. He was only going to work half days, but he was determined to go to the office every day to see his patients. He had enormous determination, courage, and perseverance, and she admired him for it.

The holidays had been difficult for him, but they had gotten through it, and despite his weakness and extreme fatigue, there was a kind of joy which pervaded every moment for Alaistair and Gabrielle. Although they couldn't see evidence of it yet, they were praying for a miracle.

Chapter 14

Christmas at Patrick Martin's home was as one would have expected. He was living in the furnished apartment he had rented, and Alice was living in their apartment. Marina came back from university for her Christmas holiday, and visited her father every day, while living with her mother. Damien had refused to see his father for the past two months and said he could no longer bear the sight of him, for his hypocrisy and his lies, and what he had done to their mother. Alice looked haggard, worn out by the strain of what they were living through. Pain, shame, humiliation, terror of what the future would bring. They were living on the rapidly dwindling money in their joint account. Patrick had used a large portion of it to pay his criminal attorney, in advance of the court proceedings, and had drained their savings to pay Sergei's blackmail.

He spoke only to his lawyers and no one else, preparing for the trial, scheduled now in February, after a brief continuance. He thought of it night and day, and was terrified that he would go to prison, and what they would do to him there. He hated Sergei Karpov with a rabid passion, for what he had done to him, in death and in life. If Sergei had still been alive, Patrick thought he might actually have killed him. He could no longer imagine any kind of future, unless he was found innocent and exonerated. But even if that happened, the public would never forget what had happened and what they had read in the newspapers. Patrick hated the media too. He was filled with hatred and a kind of obsessive poison that surrounded him like a lethal form of gas. Just being near him was poisonous.

Alice hadn't seen him, only Marina had. No one else wanted to. And Christmas was a sad affair in their family home, with Alice, both her children at war with each other over their father, and Patrick alone in his apartment, until Marina went to visit him late in the day. The holidays didn't exist for them this year. There were no presents, no warm exchange of good wishes, no expression of affection between them. It was like a house filled with death, and all because of Patrick and the toxic life he had led among the worst element of human beings. Sergei was free of his mortal life now, but Patrick carried all the burdens of his mistakes and his mortality, his sins and his lies. Every life Patrick had touched had been poisoned by him. He had no allies or supporters, no one to love him except his daughter. He twisted her mind shamefully, convincing her that he was the victim, and he had been abused and ill-used by everyone, the government, his family, the press, and especially her brother, judging him for being a homosexual while Patrick continued to be in denial about his own proclivity in that direction. He was a very sick man, filling his daughter's head with lies to his benefit, and Damien hated him all the more for it. Alice was numb watching her family disintegrate.

She had taken off her wedding ring, and was waiting to file the divorce after the trial. All the papers were ready and had been signed, and all she wanted now was to be free of him, and no longer have any tie to him. She was going to take back her maiden name with the divorce. She was on Christmas break from the Sorbonne, which was a relief.

They were a family waiting for the axe to fall, and in his delusional state, Patrick had begun to believe that he would be found innocent. He insisted that no judge could condemn him for the death of someone as worthless as Sergei. Marina didn't go back to university in Lille after the holidays. Her head was too full of everything her father was saying to her, and she couldn't leave knowing that no one would visit her father, as she did, every day.

They were living in a hell of Patrick's making. It was going to be a relief for them all when the trial started. January seemed to crawl by as they waited.

The month flew by for Gabrielle, eager to get back to Alaistair. He seemed to be doing better and getting stronger again. She spoke to Geoff frequently, who reported that he looked better too. December had been a frightening low point, but in January he showed some slight improvement. He had his last treatment in London in mid-January. She flew to Paris to meet him the day before his final treatment with Professor Leblanc. She hadn't seen Alaistair in a month, and she thought he looked better too. His color was healthier and his eyes not so sunken in his head. They seemed brighter. Leblanc was admitting him to the hospital again for the final treatment, and to run a battery of tests at the same time. Gabrielle went with him, and waited in the hallway for hours until they let her see him. He was heavily sedated and couldn't keep his eyes open or form a sentence, and he slept through until the next morning, while she dozed in the waiting room, with a pillow the nurse had given her. When she saw him in the morning, the day after his treatment, he was eating breakfast and smiling. They discharged him afterward, and the professor promised to call him with the results of the tests by the end of the week.

They stayed in Paris for two days, this time so Gabrielle could get some sleep. She was exhausted, and Alaistair wanted to pamper her. He treated her like a small child in need of motherly nurturing. He wanted to take care of her, and he knew that whatever he did would never be enough to repay her for all she had done for him. She was touched by how loving he was to her.

They spent most of their time in bed at the hotel, but went out to get some air that afternoon. Gabrielle loved looking at the shops on the Faubourg Saint-Honoré. All the best shops were there, including several Alaistair liked too. They were approaching the hotel after their walk when they saw three men carrying big black nylon bags like gym bags. They caught Alaistair's attention, and he saw three more men on motorcycles waiting as the men with the gym bags ran toward them. They'd been wearing knit hoods and caps and had come out of a jewelry store, and as it registered in his mind, he heard a shot ring out and without thinking he grabbed Gabrielle, shoved her between two parked cars, and covered her with his body.

"Stay down!" he commanded her in a harsh voice, as more shots rang out and the three men on motorcycles raced past them. Alaistair saw clearly the men on the back and the bags they were holding as the motorcycles wove through the traffic. And as he and Gabrielle crouched on the ground, what seemed like a whole brigade of police on motorcycles raced by. Alaistair poked his head up so he could see better and Gabrielle pulled him down by his jacket frantically.

"What are you doing?" Gabrielle asked him. There were no more sounds of guns being fired and when he looked again, he saw that the motorcycle police had blocked the end of the street, and reinforcements were dragging the men who'd run away off their motorcycles. Alaistair stood watching as the bags were roughly yanked from their hands and handed to other policemen, as the original three were handcuffed and shoved into police cars, with the motorcycle drivers.

"What was that all about?" Gabrielle asked, looking shaken. The sound of gunfire was unmistakable.

"I think it was a robbery of a jewelry store," Alaistair said, awestruck by what they'd just experienced. The street was still blocked and police pushed their way through passersby and told them to leave the area. He had a rapid exchange with one of the officers, and led Gabrielle down a side street away from where they'd been crouched.

"Where are we going?" Gabrielle asked as she followed him, and he pulled her along.

They reached the hotel by a circuitous route a few minutes later, and there were clusters of people outside and policemen with their guns drawn. They were allowed to go inside the hotel when they showed their key cards. People were talking about the robbery that had just occurred.

"I told the policeman where we're staying and gave him our names, if they want a statement from us," he explained to Gabrielle as they crossed the lobby and went upstairs to their room.

"I didn't see their faces, just the motorcycles speeding past us," she said, as he unlocked the door and they went in.

Two policemen came to see them that night and spent half an hour with them in the living room of the suite. Alaistair translated for her. All three of the suspects had been caught, along with their accomplices driving the motorcycles, and the jewelry had been re-covered. The police declared them amateurs and said they were part of a gang that had been attacking jewelry stores in the area for the past two months.

"Thank God they didn't attack the jewelry stores here at the hotel," Gabrielle said, still shocked by what they'd seen.

The policeman who'd taken down their statements had them each sign and wrote down their contact information and then left them. Alaistair said he was grateful that they'd been able to avoid the ex-change of fire between the parked cars.

"You never know what's going to happen," he said to her after the policemen left. The thought that she could have been injured or killed left him shaken as he put his arms around her and held her tight. He couldn't have borne losing her now. It was exactly what she was thinking about him. They were waging a life and death battle against his illness, it had never occurred to either of them that other unseen dangers could put either of them at risk. Alaistair clung to her all night, and in the morning, they read all about it in the news-papers. Six men had been arrested and were in jail. No bystanders had been injured. By some miracle, they'd been protected. And Gabrielle just hoped their luck would hold, and Alaistair would be spared from his illness too. And they were both grateful for how lucky they had been the day before. And she remembered vividly how Alaistair had covered her with his body to protect her from stray bullets. She knew she'd never forget it.

They were still in Paris when Patrick Martin's trial started and it was all over the press. The prosecutor for the state opened with the most damning statements imaginable, which were quoted in the media. He referred to the victim and the defendant as scum feeding off scum. He said that Patrick's world and career were built on lies. He said Patrick had deceived an entire country and besmirched the good name of the office he represented. Everything about the trial sounded ugly. Alaistair read about it, and translated for her. It made one cringe just reading it, and it sounded as though the atmosphere in the courtroom was as noxious as the case itself and the people involved. It was still continuing when Alaistair and Gabrielle went back to London. She decided to stay with him for another week, until they heard from the professor about Alaistair's tests. She wanted to be there when he got the call, to support him if the news was bad, or rejoice with him if there was some improvement, even if slight.

Professor Leblanc called a few days later than they'd expected. He called early in the morning, before Alaistair had left for work. Gabrielle knew immediately who it was from the look of pure terror on Alaistair's face. He stood very still holding the phone and listening, and she couldn't guess which way it had gone from what he said at his end. He looked so serious and so intent that she held her breath as she waited. She could tell from what Alaistair was saying that he wanted him to see another doctor somewhere, which didn't sound like good news to her. At the end of the call, he thanked Leblanc in a strangled voice, put down the phone, and stood staring at her. He didn't speak for a moment, he couldn't. He had tears in his eyes and he seemed so shocked that he had no words, and then finally he found his voice, as Gabrielle went to comfort him.

"He got the results of all the tests. Remission. I'm in remission . . . oh my God, Gabrielle, I'm in remission! I'm cancer-free for now. He doesn't know how long it will last, a short time or forever, but it's completely gone. I'm going to live." He started sobbing as he said it, and she held him in her arms as they stood there crying together. They had won . . . he had won . . . he had been willing to commit suicide, and instead he had fought a painful battle that nearly killed him—and won! Her legs were shaking so much she had to sit down, and he sat down next to her and held her so tightly she couldn't breathe. She couldn't think. She couldn't speak. All she knew was that he was not going to die. She thought of all the nights during Christmas when she had been terrified to close her eyes for fear he would die while she slept, and it would be over. The nightmare had ended. They had woken up.

"Oh my God," was all she could say, silently thanking God for the miracle they had prayed for but didn't think would come.

Alaistair looked at her, smiling through his tears, and he kissed her. It still hadn't sunk in. He called Geoffrey then, and he had burst into tears too. Alaistair wanted to shout it from the rooftops, but he was afraid to believe it, as though someone might take it away. He left the house looking dazed, determined to go to work and find normalcy again at last. The professor had warned him that he would feel weak for some time, from the drugs he'd taken, but his strength would return. He had to continue to have tests regularly and be monitored to make sure there was no change. He told Gabrielle before he went out that there was an important researcher the professor wanted him to see in New York. The doctor in New York would go over the data in the case, for his own interest and the benefit of his patients, and Leblanc said he would welcome the doctor's assessment of Alaistair's case as well, to offer his opinion of the test results. Alaistair was going to fly to New York with Gabrielle to see him. But whatever happened now, he was in remission. He was free! For now, for a while, or forever, they couldn't know.

They celebrated that night with dinner at their favorite pub, but they both felt like zombies, elated, dazed, frightened that it wasn't really true, numb, grateful, exhausted, happy. It was a relief to go home and climb into bed and cling to each other. They had laughed and cried alternately all day. They made love, and finally fell into a sleep of utter exhaustion, in each other's arms. He thought he had dreamed it the next day. But it was true. The miracle had happened. It was theirs, the most precious gift of all.

The trial in Paris went on for two weeks, with testimony from men Patrick had had relations with in clandestine situations. Every moment of his secret life was shrouded in lies. None of the men accused him of violence, only of dishonesty and buying their silence with bribes. Other witnesses testified to Sergei blackmailing them too, and using them financially in every way possible. It was difficult to tell who was the guiltiest and the most repulsive, the victim or the accused. There was no way to have sympathy for either of them. Alice Martin sat staunchly in the courtroom for all of it, as still as a statue, occasionally wiping a tear away with a tightly folded handkerchief, while her daughter sobbed openly, two rows away, and looked with hatred at her mother. She tried to force her way to her father at one point and finally had to be removed from the courtroom. Damien looked like a volcano about to erupt. They were a family destroyed, all by one man. As the prosecutor said, Patrick had no redeeming qualities, in his public life, or his private life, as a father, a minister of the government, as a husband, or as a man. Everything he had done was deplorable. The investigating judge had come to similar conclusions on his own. The case was to be handed off to another judge who would try the case. Patrick was being charged with involuntary manslaughter. There was no evidence that he had ever laid hands on the deceased. And if he had, it couldn't be proven. There was no concrete evidence of either his innocence or guilt of premeditated murder. He had the motive to want to kill him, but the facts of the case remained ambiguous. Patrick had risen out of his seat with a howl of pain when the prosecutor asked for a charge of first-degree murder and thirty years in prison. He sank down in his seat again when it was denied.

The verdict came finally in the third week of the trial. The defendant was ordered to stand, and because it could not be proven that he had touched Sergei Karpov to push him, Patrick was convicted of involuntary manslaughter as the result of their altercation, and given five years in prison. There was a shriek of despair from his daughter, and Patrick was crying in the silence that followed. He was convicted of fleeing the scene as well. Then the judge pronounced that because of his service to the country as minister of the interior, the sentence was suspended, with probationary supervision for the full five years. He was free, but the judge pointed out that he took with him the full burden of his crimes, and the many people he had injured by his actions, including his own children and wife. Alice had sat completely motionless while the sentence was pronounced, and never looked at him, and Damien shook his head in disgust, and put an arm around his mother.

Patrick Martin looked as though he was in shock when he left the courtroom with his lawyer to sign the documents for the suspended sentence and probationary supervision. They had been lenient with him, more than he deserved.

Marina trailed behind her mother as they left the court. They were assaulted by the press as soon as they left the courtroom, and Damien tried to shield his mother and sister. The three of them got into Damien's car and drove away. There were tears rolling down Alice's cheeks, but she didn't say a word. Damien couldn't tell if she was relieved or disappointed, if she wanted him to go to prison or not. He drove her home, and put her to bed with a glass of water beside her. She thanked him, and closed her eyes, as though she couldn't bear what she'd seen and heard anymore.

Damien hoped that his father wouldn't have the guts to come to the apartment or see any of them, at least for a while. He knew that his mother was going to file the divorce immediately, and hoped she wouldn't change her mind, but she was too shaken for him to ask her anything. He gently closed her bedroom door and left her alone to cry for her shattered life.

Chapter 15

What Patrick Martin was left with after the trial was his physical freedom, and nothing else. As a result of the conviction on manslaughter charges, he lost his license to practice law and was disbarred. His political life had ended in disgrace. He would never be able to get a job again in any of the fields he was trained for and his financial situation was not strong. He had lived off the many perks that came with his job, cars and drivers, vacation spots, subsidies for his home, and all the gifts and services people gave him for free. They were all gone now, and he had no means of finding employment, or of replacing what he had. He had no visible means of support now, except if he went to work, but doing what? His situation would become dire very quickly. And he didn't know it yet, but for compensation for the indignities and emotional abuse she suffered at his hands, Alice Martin was requesting full ownership of their apartment for her own use, and to sell at her discretion if she wished, and her lawyer thought she would get it. Patrick was a criminal now, and had no rights. If he stepped one inch over the line of the law, the suspension would be removed from his prison sentence, and he would go to prison for five years, where he was unlikely to survive among hardened criminals.

Patrick came to the same conclusions as he sat in his small furnished apartment. Three days after the trial ended, Damien was called in the middle of the night. His partner answered the phone and handed it to Damien with a woebegone expression. He thought Damien was cursed to have a father like him, and had said so to Damien.

The emergency services of the Pitié Salpêtrière were calling Damien. His father had taken an overdose of sleeping pills and was in a coma, and not expected to live. They were advising Damien in case he wished to come, but given the dose his father had ingested, they thought that his recovery from the coma was unlikely, and there had been possible brain damage. Damien's mother had filed the divorce the day before, but Patrick had not been advised of it yet, so she had no reason to feel guilty. Only Damien knew that she had filed it.

After he hung up, Damien sat quietly for a minute, and then got out of bed, and pulled on his jeans.

"What are you doing?" Achille, his partner of the past three years, asked him. Damien had recently introduced him to his mother, who had thought Achille seemed like a kind man. She was learning more about her son's life now that he had come out.

"My father tried to commit suicide. He's in a coma, and not expected to live," Damien said soberly, not sure what he felt.

"I'm sorry to say it, but after what he's done to you, and your mother, and brainwashed your sister, and everything he's done, it's his karma. Do you need to go?" Damien nodded. There were unshed tears in his eyes. He couldn't even cry for him anymore.

"I'll come with you," Achille said quietly, and hugged him as a sob finally broke from Damien.

"He's an awful person, and I know it. But he's my father. He shouldn't die alone." Achille thought it a suitable fate for him, but didn't say it. And he drove Damien to the hospital a few minutes later.

When they got there, Patrick was in a cubicle by himself. He was wearing a hospital gown. He was deadly pale, his lips were gray tinged with blue, and he was on a respirator, unable to breathe on his own. He already looked dead, but he wasn't. Damien stood staring at him for a long time, trying to feel something for him, with Achille next to him, and then he went to sit in the hallway, to wait for the end.

A doctor came to see Damien and explained that his father could be in the coma for a long time, as long as he remained on the respirator.

"You can go home. We'll call you if anything happens. We tried to reach your mother, but there was no answer and no voicemail, so we called you."

"I'm glad you did." He knew she had unplugged her landline after she filed the divorce papers, and she wasn't answering her cellphone. She didn't want to speak to Patrick once he was advised of the dissolution she had requested. The lawyer had said that Patrick wouldn't be advised about the divorce for at least five days, so he didn't know about it, and probably didn't believe she would ever file. But Damien was proud of her for doing it.

Achille and Damien went home, and in the morning, Damien went to see his mother to tell her about his father's attempted suicide. When he did, she sat staring at him. She didn't cry, or speak, she just looked at him and nodded.

"Do you want to see him, Maman?" he asked her, and she shook her head.

"I have nothing to say to him."

"He can't hear you anyway. It's just if you want to see him."

"I don't want to remember him that way." There was no way she wanted to remember him now. She wanted to erase him from her memory with the divorce. She wanted a fresh start and had been considering transferring to a university in another city where no one knew her, using her maiden name. She had already started using it before the trial, and wanted it confirmed by the court now.

It was much harder telling Marina, and she did want to see him. Damien took her to the hospital and she lay across her father's chest and sobbed until the nurses removed her so she didn't suffocate him. Then Damien took her home. He didn't try to argue with her about how she felt. She was too distraught, and Damien felt she had a right to love her father, no matter what he had done.

Their mother put her to bed and brought her a cup of tea.

"Why are you all so mean to him?" Marina sobbed. "You don't even want to see him." Her mother didn't answer her. There was too much to explain, and Marina didn't want to hear it anyway. Alice went back to her own room, but left Marina's door open, in case she needed her. She had to live with it now, and come to terms with who her father was.

Gabrielle read of Patrick Martin's attempted suicide in London, where she was still with Alaistair. He was looking and feeling better every day, and so was she. They had survived his death sentence, and now they were free.

But she was shocked to read that Patrick Martin, only days after his conviction and suspended sentence, was in a coma on a respirator after an attempted suicide. She showed the article to Alaistair and he shook his head.

"Now that is one truly bad man."

"He put his family through so much," she agreed with him. "It's strange how life works, isn't it? Do you suppose he'll die?"

"He might but he might not. People can live in those comas for a long time. He won't be the same though if he wakes up. The longer he's in it, the greater the chance of serious brain damage. So, they don't even have the relief of his being dead, after everything he put them through."

Patrick Martin awoke from the coma after three weeks. He had severe memory loss, from the enormous amount of sleeping pills he had ingested, and he had been barely alive when a neighbor found him. He had left the door open, so they would. He didn't want to be lying there dead for a month before someone discovered his body.

When he regained consciousness, he no longer had any memory

of the trial, or the sentence, or what had led to it. He remembered his name when prompted, and some details of his boyhood, and very little else. The doctor told Damien that it was unlikely he would regain consciousness, so it was a surprise when he did. But the damage was too great, and the coma had lasted too long. The doctor also told him that his father couldn't remain in the hospital indefinitely. He wasn't ill, and they needed the bed. A long-term solution had to be found for him, but there were long waits for beds in public health service facilities that would care for him. There would have to be an interim solution.

Damien spoke to Achille about it that night, and Achille wasn't happy about it.

"It won't be forever, and hopefully not even for long. He's my father. I feel as though I have to help. He's like a child now. He can't take care of himself, and there's no one else to do it."

"Your mother won't take him short-term?"

Damien shook his head. "She doesn't want to see him, and I don't want her to take him in. It's too much for her. She's been through enough. It would break her." It was a miracle that it hadn't yet. "I'm the only one who can," Damien said quietly. It would be his final gift to his father, his act of forgiveness.

"All right, but for no more than two weeks. I'll help you find a place for him. I really don't want him here, but I'm doing this for you," Achille said, sorry for him. Damien had been through a lot too.

"Thank you," Damien said, and kissed him on the cheek.

They picked Patrick up two days later, and had been promised a bed by the public health service within two weeks.

He acted like a lost child when they brought him to Damien's apartment. They had an empty spare room and a mattress, which was the best they could do. He wet the bed at night. It was an agony having him there, and they couldn't wait for him to leave. But Achille lived up to what he had promised Damien, and Damien did it as the ultimate act of charity for a father who no longer knew him. He remembered Damien's name, but not who he was, and was confused whenever he saw him.

He had been there for a week when the doorbell rang one morning. Damien was surprised to see his mother standing there. She knew what Damien was doing for his father, and was grateful for it. She knew she couldn't have. Not anymore.

"I came to see your father," she said quietly. "May I see him?"

Damien nodded and took her to the small room. Patrick was awake, and lying there in pajamas, staring at nothing. He didn't look up as Alice began to speak, and their son left them alone with each other. His mother looked like she had something to say. She spoke in a clear firm voice.

"Patrick, I came to tell you that I forgive you for all the terrible things you did to me, for what a bad father you are, to Damien, and to Marina. I forgive you for your lies and your cruelty and the terrible things you did with other men. I forgive your cowardice and dishonesty. For all your sins, I forgive you. I renounce you as my husband. I never want to see you again, but in the name of God, I forgive you." And with that she walked out of the room, as Patrick stared after her, having understood nothing. She thanked Damien and left. He left for work himself shortly after that. He had a babysitter who came every day to watch his father. He couldn't miss any more work.

He had heard what she'd said to him. He admired her for it. She was an honest woman, and deeply religious. He didn't know how she could forgive him. To her, he was dead now. The man who had been her husband was gone anyway, and no one would miss him.

Marina had finally gone back to college in Lille. She had seen him once on the respirator and that was enough. She knew he was gone. After that, she left. Damien knew she would probably go to visit him at the public health service facility now, but Patrick wouldn't know who she was, just as he didn't recognize Damien.

Patrick was a walking corpse now, an empty shell of a human being. The lies were over, and so was everything else. He barely had a brain that functioned.

He had been punished for his crimes and his sins. The slate had been wiped clean. And so had his brain and his capacity to use it. Destiny had intervened and imposed its own life sentence on him.

Chapter 16

There was another, smaller art fair in London while Gabrielle was still there, and she decided to check it out, to see if there was anything she wanted, or needed for a client. The fair was small and well done. Alaistair went with her, and enjoyed it. When they went out to dinner afterward, he asked her if she would ever consider working from London, so she didn't have to spend half her life on planes to be with him. She smiled.

"I've thought of that myself. I really need to be in New York part of the time. But I could work from here most of the time. My work is kind of a movable feast." It was a nice way to look at it, and he wouldn't mind her dividing her time, if that was what she needed to do. Her work was important to her, and he respected that, just as his was important to him. "You need to go to New York one of these days anyway, to see Dr. Thatcher, the doctor Professor Leblanc referred you to. When are you going to do that?"

"Soon. I just wanted to give Geoff a breather. He's worked for me so much in the last five months. The poor guy needs a break. I'll call the doctor in New York this week, and see when he can fit me in. Leblanc thought he'd be interested in my case, and he wants an opinion from him about how long this remission might last. Leblanc seems to think it could be for good. I'd like to hear what this man has to say about it too."

"So would I." He was gaining strength every day.

"I thought we could make that ring on your finger legal one of these days too, if I'm going to be around, and it's starting to look that way." There would always be a thin line of fear for him, and for Gabrielle too, that the nightmare would come back again. But it could happen to anyone, with no history at all, just as it had happened to him. There were no guarantees for anyone's future. We are all vulnerable, fragile beings, and life can change in an instant into something terrifying or something beautiful. No one is exempt.

He called Dr. Thatcher, the researcher in New York, the following day, and was given an appointment in two weeks. Gabrielle had to go home before that. Alaistair could join her for a long weekend.

Gabrielle went back to New York at the end of the week, and Alaistair arrived a week later. She had made more space for him in her closets by then, and moved some things around so the apartment would work better for him. She had a partner's desk in her study which they could both use.

He went to the appointment with Dr. Thatcher. He was anxious about it, and didn't sleep the night before. She had a big meeting with her Greek client she couldn't change, and Dr. Thatcher only had one open time slot for him, so he and Gabrielle had agreed he'd go alone.

"What if he sees something that Leblanc missed? Or he thinks he's wrong?" Alaistair said to Gabrielle over breakfast.

"Then we start again, just like we did before. But maybe he'll think everything's fine now, just the way Leblanc does. Why not focus on that until you hear what he has to say?" She felt badly about not going with him, but he insisted he was fine with it.

Alaistair was too terrified to speak as he sat in the waiting room before he saw him. Professor Leblanc had emailed all his records to Dr. Thatcher, for him to study before the appointment, and he had. He'd examined them diligently, and shown them to his own research partner.

He looked stone-faced when Alaistair walked into his office. His legs were shaking and he had to sit down.

"I imagine this must be stressful for you," the doctor said, glancing at Alaistair. "To get a clean bill of health from one practitioner, and ask another to have a second look. And researchers never agree." It was obvious to Alaistair that he was preparing him for bad news, and he suddenly felt sick, and as though he might faint. The doctor went on. "But in this case, I do agree. In fact, I think Dr. Leblanc was conservative in his assessment to you. I think you're clean, and cancer free. I don't see this as a remission, or an *inter*mission, I see this as a cure, assuming you continue to be cancer-free, which is crucially important data for us. Somehow, your cells and his therapy and your DNA meshed perfectly, and he hit one right out of the park. I can't imagine a better result. It may have been rough, I'm sure it was, but it was worth every miserable moment you spent with that treatment.

Congratulations," he said, extending a hand, and Alaistair shook it with tears in his eyes. He couldn't speak for a moment, he was so moved and so emotional.

"My future wife is going to be very happy to hear this. Dr. Leblanc gave us our life back. I was a dead man when I met her. I was supposed to be dead within two months."

"It looks that way sometimes. And it can happen as we predict, but sometimes we're wrong, or we find an answer that's tailor-made for that person. I personally believe in the strength of the human spirit. Sometimes you have to heal the heart and the mind and the spirit before the body will follow. That's not the kind of thing researchers like to hear." He smiled at Alaistair. "So maybe your future wife had something to do with this too, if she met you at a low point and it all changed. We don't really know entirely why it works when it does. But all you can do is grab life with both hands, swim as far as you can, fight with everything you've got. And if you're lucky on top of all that, you win." He stood up then, and Alaistair felt as though he was floating out of his office. He was waiting for Gabrielle when she came home that night. He'd called to tell her it had gone well, but he wanted to give her the details in person. She was afraid it meant bad news that he wanted to see her to tell her.

"He said that Leblanc did an outstanding job, and he agrees with everything he did. He only disagreed with one thing, which he sees as a mistake, of semantics perhaps. He doesn't see this as a remission, as Leblanc does. He sees it as a cure. He doesn't think it will come back. Time will tell, but he thinks we chased the bad guys away for good."

"Oh my God, Alaistair . . ." He saw her knees buckle before she fell and he caught her on the way down. He put her down gently on the floor and sat next to her.

"It means you really are free," she said in hushed tones, as though they were in church.

"We're done," he confirmed. "It wasn't fun, but it worked."

"You were very brave about it."

"So were you, and he said something about that too. Basically, he said that they don't know everything required to achieve a cure, but they know it takes the heart and the mind and the body. He basically said that the love of a good woman makes a big difference, so essentially you saved my life, Gabbie. I had two months to live when you met me. You changed everything. If I hadn't met you, I'd have committed suicide months ago. I didn't think I had a chance."

"Well, you did have a chance. And you won," she said, and he kissed her.

Chapter 17

I t took the social services people three weeks to find a public health service placement for Patrick Martin. It was in a small well-kept home where he had a private room, where he could be alone. At his age, he could be in the public health system for a long time. A private facility would have been better of course, but he didn't have the funds to pay for it, and none of his family members did either. The home he was in was within a reasonable distance of Paris. Relatives or even friends could visit him if they wished. So far no one had. And Marina would when she was home from school. He didn't have the capacity to recognize anyone, which usually discouraged relatives from coming eventually. All they wanted to know was that he was being well cared for, which absolved them from responsibility or guilt.

The judge in their divorce case awarded Alice Chalon ex-Martin full ownership of the apartment as a divorce settlement. She sold it and intended to buy a smaller one with a room for her daughter when she settled permanently in a new city. She had applied for teaching jobs in Reims, Bordeaux, and Grenoble, and didn't have an answer yet. And whatever money she had left over, she was going to invest as a cushion for the future. Marina had already transferred to Madrid to finish her studies. She wanted to be in a place where no one knew or cared about Patrick Martin. It was a good decision.

Richard and Judythe's baby boy was born in June, and they named him Alaistair Sam, the Sam being for the SAMU who had also saved Richard's life.

"You could have named him Louis the Sixteenth, after the hotel, which has a certain regal ring to it," Alaistair teased them at the christening. But he was touched that they had named their baby after him.

Alaistair and Gabrielle got married in a small ceremony with Veronica and Georgie present in New York in August. The girls were their mother's witnesses and Richard Sheffield was Alaistair's best man. They postponed the honeymoon for a month.

And in September, Alaistair and Gabrielle went to Paris to celebrate the anniversary of when they'd met. They stayed at the Louis XVI, in their usual suite, which was Gabbie's favorite.

They went to all the places they'd been to before, and new ones they had discovered since, on the many occasions they had gone to Paris for his treatments. They went to see Professor Leblanc to thank him personally for saving his life. He told Gabrielle again that she had been an important part of the equation, and the secret ingredient that might have made all the difference. They would never know which part tipped the balance in the right direction, but the results were remarkable. He had written several papers on his findings, and he and Dr. Thatcher had remained in close communication.

When they went back to the hotel, they saw Olivier Bateau and Yvonne Philippe, faithful to their posts, standing next to the front desk. Olivier was smiling broadly. He nodded acknowledgment to Gabrielle and Alaistair as they approached the desk. Gabrielle whispered her disapproval.

"Louis Lavalle would never have stood there like a bobble-head. He would have been across the lobby by now, shaking your hand and kissing mine, and asking how the girls are."

"And probably collecting an enormous tip, from what I've been told," Alaistair whispered back.

"Yes, but he did it with so much style and grace that nobody minded. Bateau barely says hello to us. He can't be bothered."

"My clinical assessment is that the guy is a nervous wreck, and is in way over his head, and knows it. This is the first time I've seen him smile in a year." They were at the desk by then and Bateau hadn't moved as Yvonne greeted them warmly.

"What can I do to help you?" Yvonne asked them.

"We forgot our key card in the room," Gabrielle answered, and nodded at Olivier Bateau. He always annoyed her, just the way he stood there, looking like a dog trying to hide, with his paws over his head. But this time he smiled at her.

"Have you met our new manager?" he asked them, and they looked around to see who it was. He pointed to Yvonne, who had been his assistant all year since they reopened. She essentially ran the place, and could be seen all around the hotel, while Olivier hid in his office. "Miss Yvonne Philippe. She's taking over my job, effective tomorrow."

"You're leaving?" Gabrielle was surprised. He seemed so pompous and officious to her, and so ineffective.

"I'm transferring," he said proudly. "I'm not a big city boy. I come from a small town in the mountains, in the Jura. I'm moving on to greener pastures, or quieter ones. I'll be the general manager at our ski chalet in Megève in the winter. And a small hotel we're building in Saint-Jean-Cap-Ferrat in the summer. I'm looking forward to it. And Miss Philippe will take on the mother ship right here in Paris. She's been a great help to me all year since we reopened."

Gabrielle remembered that Yvonne had been in evidence everywhere, even handing out blankets and water bottles the night of the bomb threat, while Bateau looked like he was going to faint, and couldn't get out the door fast enough, ahead of the clients. Whoever had decided to send him away had chosen the right locations. They were smaller high-end vacation spots and much less stressful. He looked like a happy man as they shook Yvonne's hand and congratulated her on the promotion. It was a big one.

As they rode up in the elevator a few minutes later, Alaistair and Gabrielle couldn't help but think back a year. It had all started with Richard's heart attack, the accidental death of a Russian blackmailer, the exposure of a major French politician leading an unsavory double life, who wound up accused of murder, was convicted of manslaughter and sentenced to prison, and the two of them meeting on the weekend that Alaistair was contemplating suicide. He would have been dead by now if Gabrielle hadn't been starting her life over, after her husband's betrayal when he ran off with what her daughters now called their step-hooker.

Gabrielle's trip to Paris to visit the Biennale had ultimately saved Alaistair's life, just as he had saved Richard's. There was no question that life was complicated. But in the complications were both the questions and the answers, the hidden solutions and unexpected blessings. All one needed was the courage to pursue them. In the end, the complications they had run into had served them well. And whatever the answers and the solutions, and no matter how hard the road, every day was a gift.

As they got off the elevator on the third floor, the fire alarm went off, reverberating through the building. Gabrielle and Alaistair looked at each other and laughed.

"Happy anniversary!" he said to her over the din and kissed her, as they headed toward the stairs to exit the building yet again.

When they got to the lobby, as guests continued to pour out of their rooms and down the stairs, Yvonne and two assistants were apologetically informing everyone that it was a false alarm. Olivier Bateau was nowhere in sight.

"It's never boring when we stay here," Alaistair commented, and Gabrielle laughed as they waited for the elevator.

"Nothing is boring with you." Their life for the past year had been an extraordinary adventure, and every precious moment, even the hardest, was a gift.

Danielle
Steel

Have you liked Danielle Steel on Facebook?

Be the first to know about Danielle's latest books,
access exclusive competitions and stay in touch
with news about Danielle.

www.facebook.com/DanielleSteelOfficial

THE BUTLER

Everything happens for a reason . . .

Joachim and Javier von Hartmann were born into a wealthy Argentine banking family. But when facts emerge of their grandfather's wartime activity, both boys and their mother, Liese, are cast out from the family. After the years of glamour and luxury, she must raise them alone. While Javier descends into criminality, Joachim moves to England to become a butler for the wealthy. When he travels to Paris to spend some time with his mother, he finds that there's no call for butlers there. However, he gains a job as assistant and confidant to Olivia, an American who needed to escape her life in New York.

Both Joachim and Olivia hold secrets about their past, and as reports come through that Javier's life in the Colombian underworld is spiralling out of control, they must make difficult decisions. What they come to understand is that destiny has a hand in their future and everything that came before had a reason. The future will unfold as it was meant to and they will face it together.

Coming soon

PURE STEEL. PURE HEART.